Us Ones
In Between

Us Ones
In Between

By
Blair Mastbaum

RUNNING PRESS
Philadelphia • London

ISBN-13: 978-1-60751-273-8

Edited by Don Weise
Cover Designed by Scott Idleman
Interior designed by Jan Greenberg
Typography: Giovanni, Bodega Sans, Badhouse

Running Press Book Publishers
2300 Chestnut Street
Philadelphia, PA 19103-4371

"I've heard of pious men

And I've heard of dirty fiends

But you don't often hear

Of us ones in between."

—Spencer Krug, Sunset Rubdown

TABLE OF CONTENTS

Chapter One

The Urge to Push

Lying in bed, tired and sweaty because it's so hot, I think about my name. It's so mundane. Kurt Smith. Why couldn't my parents have named me something interesting like Liam or Alcott or Barclay? I guess my first name isn't that bad because I share it with one of my idols — Kurt Cobain — but my last name, come on. If you looked me up on the Internet, the only result you'd get (that's actually me) is one art exhibit posting from a show I was in when I was still a painting major at Cooper Union three years ago. Pathetic.

I live alone in the East Village in that studio apartment you picture about when you fantasize about being a fledgling novelist and living in a small, dimly lit room and drinking Scotch in the evenings, reflecting on what you'd written that day. My third-floor walk-up has an iron-stained bathtub, a kitchen sink, an old desk, and a single bed in the same small room. Out the three windows, you can see two identical four-story red brick buildings across the street. Inside, my banged up wooden door has six different locks lining its edge, even though the door to the building also locks. I guess they're leftover from the '70s when this neighborhood was scary, or cool, depending on who you talk to. The locks on my door are just to keep out the creepy neighbors like Jim, the fat guy who basically never leaves and randomly screams nonsense words in the middle of the night. Those locks can't keep out the profound emptiness of the human soul, though. Ha.

All I own are several hundred yellowed paperback books, an old iPod, a schoolteacher desk, a bed with sheets I wash twice a year, a thrift store table that wobbles, a couple of moth-eaten second-hand flannel blankets, a shitty bicycle, a partially ripped poster of the original cover of *Catcher in the Rye*, and a framed 11x14-inch photograph of a skinny, beautiful dark-haired kid with caramel-colored eyes. I don't know who he is — I found the photo in a thrift store — but I imagine that he's my all-time favorite literary character come-to-life, a distant boy named Calhoun, a junkie, from my all-time favorite novel, *American Daze* by Colin Sennerty. I imagine Calhoun to be a much cooler and more delicate version of this asshole Russian kid, Vaslov, who lives one floor below me and always wears a tracksuit jacket that says WIG-GER across the front, the WIG on one side of the zipper and the GER on the other side. It's so lame.

I moved to New York for art school when I was 18, just out of high school in the suburbs of Columbus, Ohio. My parents were alcoholics, but not that bad. They didn't hit me or fall down drunk on the front lawn. My dad was an engineer for a military sub-contractor and my mom was a media person for the Air Force. My dad loved his Audi hatchback and drove around the empty K-Mart parking lot at night like he was a racecar driver. He did donuts when it snowed, spinning around and around, barely missing the streetlight posts. My mom smoked a lot of cigarettes and got mean when she drank. When I turned vegetarian at fifteen (I dropped that after I got tired of tofu burgers), my dad got high and mighty and told me that vegetables felt pain, too. I rolled my eyes and he dropped his bottle of Scotch and blamed it on me. It shattered on the kitchen floor. My mom couldn't be bothered to clean it up — she just ashed her menthol cigarette in the sink as she watched him cut his hand on a shard of boozy glass. The blood stained the wood floor. I'm sure the blotch has been scrubbed away, but I'll never see it because my parents are divorced and don't live there anymore. And even if they did, I wouldn't want to go back to that house anyway. It's not like I have fond memories of it like most people do of their childhood homes.

I hardly ever left the basement of that big house, where I hung out with my two best friends: Sven, a skinny Swedish kid with skin the color of banana pudding who moved to Ohio for his dad's job, and Steve, who was constantly pushing his long hair from his eyes and strategically pushing it back over his eyes with the same stroke of his hand that he pushed it away with. I don't know why, but both Steve and Sven were unpopular at school. I thought it was crazy that no one liked them, because they were perfect, and they were contemporary, meaning they had little to no relationships with their families. I guess they are why I have an embarrassing and seemingly inexhaustible fetish involving skateboarders, like even if there's a skateboard sitting behind a kid, I cum faster. It's really stupid.

There in the basement, we'd smoke pot, drink vast amounts of Robitussin DM, and sometimes jack off sitting around on the big sectional sofa while watching something mindless on television like QVC. We didn't have porn or we would have watched that. They had to use their imaginations to conjure an image to shoot to, sometimes even mouthing out the names of girls from school. I just looked to my right and left at each of them. We were always shirtless down there. It was one of our traditions, probably because it was the same temperature in that basement no matter what the season, and there were no windows to let in natural light. Being in the basement made days and nights blend together until the weeks became months, and then it was time to graduate from high school and we'd successfully avoided most of the assholes we went to school with. And we got pretty creative down there, too. We formed an art collective called the Smoker Fox Club, which involved sitting around a baseball hat with a fox on it, smoking pot, and eating large amounts of cheese. We painted together, too. We called the paintings triplets — one by each of us — and they were good.

I went on to get a full scholarship for painting at Cooper Union, so my parents sort of had to pay for my New York apartment since they were getting a free pass on tuition. Also, they were probably thrilled to see me leave. In my painting classes, I

developed a style — realism mixed with impression-
ism — and made paintings of teenage boys' bed-
rooms, with each object inside totally carefully
drawn, but never a person in sight. I painted my par-
ent's old basement a lot, too, the one where I spent
all my spare time in high school. The paintings took
weeks to get right and I would usually feel like I was
losing my mind while I was working on them. But I
stopped drawing and painting after college, mostly
because I couldn't afford the paint and I had no
space. Also, I just didn't know how to go out and
network and make small talk with a bunch of lame
people at a bunch of pretentious parties that I was
supposed to attend if I was ever going to be a well-
known artist in New York. It's like you have to turn
into a little one-man business to become successful.
The work's not enough, unless you're lucky enough
to get a friend to help you out and I never did. I still
don't know what I'm supposed to say when people
ask why I gave up painting. It sort of gave me up. Was
I supposed to just keep slaving away by myself? Was
I supposed to act like I was onto something important when I knew I wasn't?

Instead of painting, I bought an old green bike on
Craigslist and rode around and looked at things, so

at least I could make something cool-looking in my imagination. I was into this whole *physical is more real than conceptual* phase, or whatever. Like I thought I should start working out and getting some muscles and stop being such a whiney, creative little fuck. That lasted about one weekend. I'm too lazy. But I still love to ride my bike. It makes me forget about my worries.

My parents stopped paying my rent three years ago, right after I graduated. My bike has a flat tire right now. So now I'm stuck home a lot writing. I write a lot about the subway system. It's totally fascinating to me, even though it's slow and dirty and it has all the charm of a Soviet work camp. When I'm down there, I lean over the tracks and peer down the tunnels trying to spot the signals and the track changes. I even love service advisories, and the signs posted up that tell you what trains aren't working properly or which one are skipping stations or temporarily running express or whatever.

I sit at my desk every day and try to write down what I'm thinking about,and then I spend most of my day trying to work on whatever novel I'm writing at the time. In reality, what this amounts to is the beginnings of a bunch of novels — six, each one a little over 100 pages and each one stopped, cut-off, abandoned, printed out and stacked in the deep bottom drawer of my desk, the drawer I never open. The characters are frozen, some mid-sentence, one eating spaghetti for all time, one riding his bike down Ludlow Street on his way to go drink beer for the rest of his life, one cumming for eternity, one considering killing himself until the end of time, one crying — forever crying. That tear on his cheek, it might not ever move again.

It's really depressing that I can't finish anything. I never thought of myself as that kind of person, even though as I look back — guitar lessons, skateboarding, even modern dance for like a month — I never finished or devoted myself enough to get good at anything I started. My half-finished novels and my journals filled with art project ideas stack up around me like tombstones and when I look at them, I feel like my throat is closing. It's pure suffocation — being smothered by my own unfinished ideas.

My current novel is about how I have the urge to push boys that I find cute or sexy or cool in front of subway trains. I don't understand exactly why I want to push them and it's not like I sit around in my apartment and think about actually doing it, but when I'm down there and some dude stands in front of me, some unattainable cool boy that I know won't acknowledge me, I really do have a strong urge to push him. The novel is called *Push*. I imagine the cover of the printed novel, even though chances are it will never be published, the letters P, U, S, and H in colored circles just like the real subway lines, my name at the bottom. In reality, only the S is a real subway line and it's just a shuttle from Times Square to Grand Central Station, but hardly anyone will think about that.

***

Elliot Collinsworth finally did it.

It involved a boy around seventeen with field mouse brown hair and pale white skin. He was carrying a scuffed-up green skateboard with red wheels, worn and chipped from the filthy cement of New York City. He was stoned, which made it easier for Elliot to sneak up behind him without him noticing, until finally, as an F train approached a decrepit Brooklyn subway station under an abandoned church, Elliot found the courage to push.

As he pushed, he felt a warm moistness through the kid's paper-thin black T-shirt, and with his delicate sense of smell, he picked up the scent of sweat mixed with Right

Guard, mixed with cigarettes. He savored this rare combinations of scents as long as he could, as this perfectly imperfect boy, this floppy creature, arched back, and one of his big-sneakered feet levitated above the grimy cement of the station like he was flying, until finally, arms flailing, he landed hard on the tracks, screaming, desperate, trying to stand up and get out of the way before the train hit him. On the platform, his skateboard rolled slowly toward the stairs, like it was being ridden by a ghost.

Elliot took five steps backward, slowly, calm, as he watched the kid fall and try to stand up, his breath held.

The train, hundreds of tons of steel and glass, barreled over him, slicing his legs off instantly.

He screamed in agony that sounded so close to euphoria, it was like an orgasm.

The train grinded to a stop.

A line of blood tricked down the cement canal between the rails.

Elliot ducked down to see the blood between the cars, savoring the view.

"Help me," the boy said in agony. He could barely talk. No one else was in the station to help him.

A subway station had never been so quiet.

Elliot peered around the station. He was totally alone. He walked toward the boy's skateboard and reached down *to pick it up as he started up the stairs. He held the skate-board close to his side like he cherished it, and he climbed up the stairs quickly and darted around the corner to catch a train back to Manhattan.*

He wasn't shaking like he thought he would be; he wasn't even scared. He felt like he wished he always felt: confident, in control, powerful.

* * *

I have to stop writing. I'm sweating and horny and exhausted. My laptop feels so hot, it seems like it might catch on fire. I push my dirty hair up and lean back in my squeaky desk chair, picturing the skater, trying to imagine him shirtless, in plaid boxers, the hair on his legs, the spine running up the back of his neck like marbles beneath his skin, a tattoo of a dragon on his shoulder. Of course he doesn't exist outside of my imagination, so that makes him more perfect than any real human boy ever could be. I bet he had that *sweetness*, that naïve happiness that everyone loses after age twenty-one or so when you realize you're not going to become someone impor-tant, the kind of innocence that can't be faked unless you're like, retarded or maybe heavily medicated. I think about being the last person on earth to touch this kid before he dies. It would feel profound, that last moment, the last touch he'd ever feel, the last human interaction ever.

I would give everything I have to get my novel published. Assuming I finish it, it would make the last year or two of being home alone and lonely so worth it, so meaningful in retrospect, but there's a part of me that knows the reality of the matter is that it'll probably just wind up in a dusty drawer along with my novel about a surfer kid in Hawaii, and with the one about the rich kid going crazy, and the one about a family who loses their dog at Yellowstone.

When I can't write anymore — times like now — I ride the subway aimlessly, trying to get in touch with what it would feel like to really do what my character, Elliot Collinsworth, does. I walk up casually behind random unsuspecting guys, trying to smell them, trying to gather some sort of telling detail about these strangers from just standing a couple feet behind them. Then I imagine how it would feel to push them, to see their crumpled bloody bodies mowed over by a train.

God, my heartbeat goes crazy just thinking about it. I break out in a sweat. I have to run away from them sometimes, literally run away. The urge to push feels *important* somehow, like I'm denying fate by not doing it, disobeying an order from some dark commander.

I avoid this feeling if I don't leave my apartment very much, even during the current brutal heat wave, which has been going on for three days and is expected to last another week.

Don't get the wrong idea. I'm not some psycho with glazed-over eyes and a missing tooth like I might picture if someone told me this story. I'm twenty-five and I look like every other pseudo-poor New York City artist, you know — underfed, skinny jeans, a T-shirt from the Staten Island Marathon 1987 that was left on the sidewalk in front of my apartment building, floppy brown hair that hangs over my eyes when I don't push it back, a necklace with a small padlock hanging from it, only as a joke though, not to be like Sid Vicious or some wanna-be. It's just an inside joke with every other person who's like me, who gets that life isn't to be taken seriously or you'll turn straight and boring and lose your edge like what's happening to the city itself. You'll have kids, and end up being one of those exhausted-looking people trying to carry one of those massive Bugaboo strollers up the subway stairs while everybody else breezes past. You'll want to be cool more than you've ever wanted it before, and the irony is, you'll never be cool again.

Okay, enough of thinking about those grim circumstances.

I have a tattoo of a roadrunner on my calf, not the cartoon character, but the real bird, like an old-fashioned line drawing, because my friends in high school used to call me roadrunner since I was always late and running to class. Right above the tattoo, I've got a big scab from the last time I rode my bike; my foot slipped and the pedal ripped open the skin on my calf. I crashed into the curb, which popped my tire. The bike still sits in the hallway outside my apartment, tire still flat.

Now the light brown hairs of my calf are coming up through a thick dark red scab that I try to tear off nearly every night. I only stop when the pain gets too sharp, when a watery bloody substance begins to seep out and tears come to my eyes.

I have a couple of friends, dudes that were in the painting department at Cooper with me, but saying *friends* is really stretching the meaning of the word. It sure as hell isn't *I believe in you* bullshit, come-live-in-my-loft-for-free-because-you're-broke-and-practically-suicidal kind of shit, although I would appreciate the offer.

One of them, my only *actual* friend I guess, the only person I see with any regularity, is a painter represented by David Zanig, the proprietor of one of the city's most prestigious galleries. His name's Sherlock, and he's a Satanist, at least that's what it says in his press bio. He likes the aesthetic anyway, of suburban teenage boys sacrificing chickens by drainage ditches and shit like that. He used to have a Mohawk, before every dork had one, when it required someone brave and confident to pull it off. Anyway, it's long since gone now that he's on the rise and I hardly ever see him anymore.

I guess he's got too much money and too many important friends and colleagues to stop by this tiny mouse-infested shithole of an apartment. He probably doesn't even remember, or has chosen to forget, how to find his way to the L train stop from his enormous loft in Williamsburg. He takes black Towncars around town. He'll wait for a car to show up for an hour, even though as I've told him 100 times, the subway would be ten times faster to Manhattan. His paintings sell for more money than my dad made in a year. Yoko Ono has one. The famous art collector

Charles Saatchi has two. There's a book on his work being planned. It's called *Teenage Wreck and Heart*. The title is perfectly evocative of nothing, just like everything young artists are creating these days.

They're beautiful, his paintings — realistic, representational, and abstract at the same time. They usually depict his friends. He did one of me posing on my bike. It was cool, but I thought he made me look sort of crazy, like insane asylum crazy. He sold it to some gallery no one's ever heard of in Germany. The place doesn't even have a website. One of the paintings is of my ex-boyfriend Billy, shirtless, reclining on this messy bed in a teenage-boy-looking bedroom, a poster of another shirtless boy on the wall behind him. That one sold to some rich gay hedge fund dude who lives in Connecticut, probably because Billy is so beautiful more than anything else.

Of course, Sherlock didn't offer it to me, even though he knows I'm still in love with Billy — he says "obsessed" — but I don't see what's wrong with it. I think obsession is beautiful, or at least honest, when very else little is. He said having Billy peering down at me 24/7 would make me even crazier. I was thinking he'd be like my Mona Lisa, his eyes watching everything I do.

Billy seems to exist solely to torture me. I know I'm overreacting, but it sure does seem like it sometimes. Like he's teasing me, hanging his life out on display so I can see every move he makes without ever being there. He goes out nearly every night with this group of stupid hipster dudes that all call each other "Fred," and they make out with each other, take their shirts off for no apparent reason, get obscenely drunk, and partake in general frat boy type partying behavior while always happening to be right in front of some club photographer's lens at exactly the right time. The photos inevitably end up on those photo-blogs online, where all those kids in their overly affected outfits pose like they don't have a care in the world. Fuck them.

Billy plays guitar in this stupid band, On the Wings of Love. They just sort of exploded this summer — at least in New York. He only knows ten chords, so he can't write music. There's some other older guy for that. Billy's way more into the *image* of being in the band than actually *being* in the band, but he'd never admit this. He acts like he's creating fine art when he talks about "his" music. When we lived together, he used to complain about not wanting to go to practice all the time. I don't know why

I'm still hooked on him, but I am and there's nothing I can do about it right now. He's got this weird but amazing energy. He can captivate a whole party just by making fun of something everyone is in love with, like Haruki Murakami or the Strokes or, I don't know, like some porn star everyone thinks is hot like that Czech dude with the blue eyes. When On the Wings of Love plays, every girl and boy in the audience is staring straight at Billy. Believe me, I know. It used to make me insane with jealousy.

Checking out Oh My Rockness, this website that lists when and where bands are playing around New York, it says that Billy has a show in a couple days. I really want to go, but I don't know if I'll have the guts to. I know it will only make me depressed for days.

My only other friend is my neighbor Jody. She's like 35 and always on a diet because she says she's afraid of becoming a fat old lady. Right now she's on South Beach. She's way too nice to me, but it feels good having someone just be cool and funny when the whole rest of the world is so difficult to deal with. She faithfully reads all of my writing and endlessly encourages me, but her support is a little sketchy because she's never not liked anything. Everything is "so amazing, Kurt!" She works for an advertising agency, and she's out of town constantly. She hasn't had a boyfriend in like two years because she's never home, and I think she sort of thinks of me as her fake boyfriend; she likes having me around so she has a dude to hang out with when she wants some dumb masculine energy around that I can fake well enough to appease her. She falls in love with these 15- to 18-year-old model boys on every shoot and then gets all upset when they stop texting her after the job's over and she's not the source of their paychecks anymore. She's pretty clueless in that way.

I don't really know why she does the things she does. She makes stupid decisions all the time, like keeping her apartment in this shithole building when she could afford something so much nicer. She seems to get off on the idea that she's living with the cast of *Rent* or something even though there are just as many yuppies in the East Village as there are weir-does and bohemians or whatever, and they're only staying because they're locked into cheap rent-controlled apartments.

Anyway, here I sit alone, one more night. With nothing to do, I've looked out my window onto Avenue B a billion times already, just watching everyone going out and walking in and out of bars and restaurants, as if this will improve my mood in some way. It's so the opposite. It's total torture watching all those people with friends laughing and talking and going places I can't afford.

Even though it's already dark, it must still be almost 90 degrees outside and totally muggy. I can't remember the last time I felt cool, clean, and dry. It's even worse because I'm depressed. Hot summer weather encourages depressed people to be happy and run outside with a fucking beach ball instead of supporting their sadness like the dead of winter does. I mean, if I had friends to go lay in the park with, to go see a show with, to walk around the art gallery openings and drink as much of the free wine as possible, that kind of thing with, maybe summer wouldn't feel so dismal.

Jody is out of town until tomorrow on a Dolce & Gabbana shoot. I'm sure she'll be nursing six different crushes on the models when she gets back. Her friend Pete, who's been around more and more lately, is staying at her place. Jody and me and him played Clue DVD the other night and I noticed that Pete, like, looked at me a little too much for a normal human being, at least the ones I know, meaning he must like me.

He just lost his rent-controlled apartment to condo-ization. While he was in the bathroom, Jody confirmed that he digs me, but I don't know what to think of him. For one, he's *bi* or whatever, at least that's what he says, but Jody thinks he's just saying this to sound more, I don't know, manly. I've known him off and on for a couple months because he used to pet-sit Jody's cat Angie before it died two weeks ago. He's sort of a wreck — he has a tragic quality that he doesn't know about. He's a writer for this lifestyle/fashion/exercise type men's magazine called *Monsieur*, which makes him totally conflicted all the time because he wants to write fiction and be cooler and less corporate and blah, blah, blah. And he's bigger than me, like he does yoga or something and maybe goes to the gym, so he's sort of got muscles, not big ones, but it's still weird because none of my friends think about their bodies like that — they wouldn't even consider working out because they're too busy hoping they look like they're too busy thinking about something arty and complex and obscure. He doesn't have any tattoos either, not that you can see anyway, and his dark brown English-schoolboy-looking hair is always combed, like he probably takes a shower every day and gets expensive haircuts in the Meatpacking District or something. He wears a tie to work — probably an expensive one, if you know what I mean. I've seen him on his way to work and I didn't know whether to laugh or sort of think he was badass for getting away with being an adult. It's just not my scene.

He does have this dark sense of humor though, which is pretty cool. That's about all that saves him. He tells jokes about abortion and rape, subjects that most people think are taboo, but totally shouldn't be, at least in my world.

Sherlock thinks he's a fag, but then he's sort of the type who thinks everyone is. I think he's straight actually, so I don't know why I even bother thinking about the possibility of kissing him or whatever. They're totally useless thoughts, a total waste of time. Sherlock mentions him all the time when he's over here and calls him Clark Kent. It's almost like Sherlock has some sort of secret crush on him.

Pete laughs and holds his arms out like Superman, always down for anything even though he probably knew we were sort of making fun of him.

I wish sometimes he wouldn't be such a good sport. I wish he'd tell Sherlock to go fuck off with his stupid cadre of artsy faggotry victims. I wish he'd get pissed off and tell me what a loser I am, but he just smiles.

I've got to stop wasting my time thinking about Pete and concentrate on my own writing now. I swear, I waste at least fifty minutes out of each hour just thinking useless shit about people I know, going over what they said the night before over and over, sometimes saying what they said out loud, determining if it was funny, pretending that I'm inside their minds. I have to finish something for once.

I slouch forward on my old leather upholstered desk chair that I found on the street during a blizzard. Once I dragged it upstairs into the heat and the snow melted on the chair, it smelled like wet dog for a month. I take a deep breath. It's too hot to think and I can't afford an air conditioner. I'm one of those annoying people who says they don't like the fake cold dry air of A/C but fuck, it would feel good about right now. There's no breeze whatsoever. My back is sticking to the leather chair. I've never been so hot and I'm practically naked — the only thing I have on is a pair of green and white Miller Genuine Draft boxer shorts with the Mexican version of the beer on them. Billy bought me these boxers from a thrift store for twenty-five cents after his band practice. He wrapped them in newspaper and wrote my name with a heart around it. He left the price tag on. I remember opening the package while sitting on the threadbare Chinese rug, the same one I have now, and I was so touched by this simple gesture because I knew he had thought about me while he was standing in the Salvation Army or whatever. As I sat there, he was strumming his guitar, watching me. I remember thinking he wasn't a very good guitarist, but that he'd improve if he kept at it. You think the people you love can do anything. Nope. He still strums those same ten chords with only the slightest sense of rhythm. I don't know why the brainwashed, allegedly youthful populace of Brooklyn got so stoked on his band all of a sudden. Their songs are so meaningless. It's just like the same chord over and over again with boring lyrics about the typical shit — love and breaking up and falling in love again. It's feel-good music, too, which I hate.

I try as hard as I can to stop thinking about him. It's not fun like a crush. This is torture because he's practically forgotten I exist and every pseudo-hipster doofus in town wants to make out with him now that his stupid band was on the cover of the fucking *Time Out*

New York and his record got a fucking nine point something on Pitchfork. The worst part is that he loves the attention, totally thrives on it, like he needed it all along and was never able to really be Billy without it. Like this was something I could never give him enough of, no matter how hard I tried.

I sometimes just really wish I was dead, but I don't have the guts to kill myself. Knowing this, Sherlock says, contributes to my general unhappiness. No kidding. Whenever I tell him about my suicidal feelings, he suggests that I join a life drawing class or pay a fucking Internet dating service to find some stranger for me to make out with. "It'll pass," he says, like he knows. He so doesn't know. How could he? He's the happiest artist I've ever met. Artists are supposed to be depressed. That's why I could have made a brilliant one. Once (and he was drunk when he said it after I'd been particularly annoying) he told me I should just go ahead with it and get the pills or the gun and take off into the sunset like Kurt Cobain. Sometimes I feel like everyone would be hugely relieved if I just went through with it. How'd I end up being this person at twenty-five? I'm the male version of some annoying cat lady, but without the pets to cheer me up, the ultimate depressing stereotype.

The first boy I ever liked beat me up. His name was Ben. He just flipped one day out of the blue, just totally went crazy. I always thought he looked like a wolf and then one day, he turned into one — a rabid one. He was even drooling.

We were hanging out and talking in the back of his pickup truck, which was parked in a cornfield about an hour outside of Columbus. The corn was like six feet tall, so we parked on a small dirt road in the middle of the field — one of the most isolated places you could possibly be in the flat Midwest. The sky had those puffy white clouds that look so pure and clean in the summer, like that old electronic song about the puffy clouds.

Ben had his hands down my pants. I tried to get into his pants to grab his boner, but I couldn't because his belt was so tight. The belt buckle made a metallic click as I tried to unfasten it. Right as it made that sound — that fast — he totally flipped out, like he had this in him all along, this potential energy waiting for the perfect moment to turn kinetic, triggered by this stupid sound. Who knows why? We'd sucked each other off like three or four times before, usually in my basement after school, so it wasn't me trying to get his pants off for the first time that made him change. He was abused by his uncle when he was younger and he said that sometimes certain things made him go crazy and he didn't know why. Well, I guess the uncle was big on getting Ben's belt off, because it was a major trigger — that metal clank — that stupid metallic blah of a sound.

He stood up, tightened his belt back as fast as he could, then, with all of his force, he punched me. The pain took a second to register, like I couldn't believe this was actually happening to me. Once I did feel it, instead of hurting in a bad way, it sort of felt good. He made my lip bleed, the iron taste of the blood tasted so similar to kissing him, it made a visceral connection that I don't think I've ever gotten rid of. Blood is like this private entrance into another person. You get it a little with cum and I'm not into getting pissed on, but blood is like the essence of someone in just a couple of drops. I guess that's why I'm still talking about him.

Then he looked at me, terrified, like he didn't know why I was bleeding, like he had returned to his body right then and there. He pushed me out the back of his truck and peeled out, leaving me stranded in the cornfield. The dust made my eyes sting and helped me start crying. The crying felt good, like I somehow deserved to get punched the whole time. It took four hours to walk home. Since I didn't have my shirt and it was an eighty-five-degree summer day, I got sunburned bright pink.

Ben never called me again. He dropped out of school two weeks later after not showing up for ten days, causing widespread rumors of him ODing. I knew he didn't do drugs except for weed, but I couldn't tell anyone, because almost no one knew we were even friends, much less that we fooled around. It felt like he died, the suddenness of his absence, and I took it hard wondering if I'd ever meet anyone that I liked that much again. I thought about him at night, imagined he was lying in my bed with me. I could smell his warm peppery scent on the T-shirt that he'd left at my house.

Losing him forever was the strangest, most alienating feeling I've ever experienced. For all I know, he really is dead. I miss him still. I think about the two or three times that he stayed over at my house and we slept together in the same bed and in the morning, we would just stare at each other's faces, lying there sideways on the pillows, and it was the most comforting feeling by a longshot that I'd ever felt up to then. It was an intense time for me. I had no one to talk to. Even if I had, no one would understand. Having to keep these feelings bottled up made my grief seem impenetrable and suffocating. I felt totally misunderstood by everyone I knew. It was my first enormous, incomprehensible loss. I'd bite my lip sometimes to make it bleed. The physical pain made the emotional pain less intense. I knew it was psycho, but it reminded me of Ben the last time I saw him.

I have to get out of this mood now, or I won't be able to even lift my arm. I go on the Internet and find a kid — shirtless, sort of hot, you know, skinny but with some muscle, and flipping off the camera, someplace in California or Florida, palm trees and beach in the background. I go to the next photo and his arms are behind his head and his surf shorts are pulled down and he's half-hard, and in the next one, he's all the way hard and stroking and that's all I need. But I can't cum no matter how hard I try. I get sore and raw and I have to give up, no matter how badly I want to get off.

I lean back, sweaty, my ears ringing. No one will ever want to fuck me and no one will ever understand me and I'm just getting older and stupider and more fucked up and more incapable of dealing with it.

Stop, I tell myself. You have to stop.

I decide to call Sherlock, because I've been alone in my apartment for like nine days and I can't remember not being stuck inside. I dial his cell phone number, all ones and twos. It's called a vanity number and he pays extra for it.

He answers. "What's up, Kurt? I'm busy, so make it fast."

Why does he have to be such an asshole? As soon as I hear his voice, I know he's not going to give me what I need. "Sorry, I just thought, maybe you'd want to come over tonight. I feel really fucked up. I was thinking about Ben and Billy."

"Dude, I can't come over tonight. I'm hosting that Smiths night in Bushwick. I could possibly swing by tomorrow on my way to the gallery. I have a meeting with some magazine editor. I asked her to come to my studio, but she won't make the trek."

Brooklynites act like it's a hassle to come to Manhattan now. I knew this would eventually happen.

"Okay. But please try. I really need to see someone. My dick is raw and my brain is dead, you know what I mean?"

"Yeah dude. Okay. Remember to eat, okay? And don't buy drugs or something stupid like that." He coughs up a lung.

"Where would I get the money to buy drugs? Are you sick or something? You sound bad."

"I think so. Well, I'll try my hardest to stop by around noon tomorrow. Bye, dude." He hangs up before I even say goodbye, probably because he senses that I wasn't going to let him off the hook so easily. Sometimes I think I should just fall in love with Sherlock. He wouldn't even have to know. It could be my pathetic secret.

I suck in my stomach and take a deep, deep breath. I have to do this by myself. It's not as if I have no self will. I pull on some pants and a T-shirt and I walk outside. My block is mostly delis and pizza places, and there's a closed-down yuppie wine bar. I laughed when I saw that that business venture failed. Around the corner, I pass a tiny gallery that shows mostly Japanese-looking anime kind of shit and a couple more new restaurants that I could never afford to eat at. I turn on my iPod to some overly dramatic classical music that Sherlock emailed me last year and finally get to the huge black cube sculpture on Astor Place — it's actually called *Alamo*, but the name doesn't make any sense. I kneel down on the sidewalk in the shadow of the cube, balancing on one corner, built by the artist so that it spins around

if you push it. It's sitting on a cement island surrounded by a constant rush of cars. I don't know
why, but the cube makes me feel better. Watching
some teenage boys laughing as they spin it around,
watching them experiencing simple joy, makes me
feel like maybe tomorrow will be okay — maybe
even tonight. The cube was the first element of New
York that caught my eye when I came here as a high
school student to visit Cooper Union. That cube
symbolized the New York of my fantasies and it still
delivers. It's thrashed up but graceful. It belongs to
everyone and no one. It just seems permanent, like it
will be here forever, even though I know it won't.

Chapter Two
Alone
for
One More
Second

I'm unemployed, if you want to call it that. It's by choice, though...sort of. Up until two months ago, I worked for a month and a half as a copyeditor at a "house and home" magazine. It sucked, obviously. Jody's friend got me the job. The office of *Superior Living* was all Martha Stewart wanna-be women, always rushing around the beige office in heels and an assortment of Easter egg-colored clothes. How I got hired, I'll never know.

I came in most days stoned, and it didn't take long for one of them to catch me looking at this photo-blog that happened to have a lot of shirtless boys and girls on it. I was just looking for Billy (I found him), but this woman thought I had a boner or something, so she could never look at me again. Interior design women hate the idea of an erection. After that, she only talked to me through my tasteful beige cubicle walls.

Anyway, I got fired not because of the website incident, but because I edited a piece about the so-called

Queen of Fabulous, the editor-in-chief of *Visage*, Edwina Halpert's minimal Amagansett beach house all wrong on purpose. I was hungover and sick of this stupid magazine making normal women all over America jealous of some rich bitch in New York City. In the copyedit, I changed the word *fashion* to *fascist*, the word *right* to *reich*, as in third. I was stoned so it seemed funny at the time. The edits made it as far as an Internet version of the story before someone caught them. They'd already printed 10,000 copies of the magazine. Supposedly Edwina Halpert was furious, totally livid when she saw her advance copy. I guess I was trying to get fired. Besides, I was tired of having to hold my arms down tight to my sides all day because I thought someone would smell me. I'm definitely not cut out for an office.

The only good part of that job is that now I get $263 a week in unemployment, at least for another month or so. After I pay my rent, that leaves me $348.50 to live on, which would be excellent if I lived in Bangladesh. And my parents are almost no help. They're all *tough love* and *get a job writing poetry* and *put all that anger to good use*. I told them none of my friends have jobs and they just looked confused.

I turn on my computer to look for Billy on more

photo-blogs. It only takes twenty seconds this time and there he is from last night at a bar called Fun in Williamsburg, holding hands with some dude I've never seen before, some dumb kid with a faux-hawk and about twenty necklaces of all lengths and materials from gold to hemp to beads. Pathetic. At the first party, he's looking all scruffy and popular. He's a fucking celebrity, at least in that incestuous little universe. His band's music is the soundtrack of the summer. I go to his MySpace and his photo is updated like every four minutes. It's him standing in his underwear, drinking a beer. Fucker. He doesn't even like beer. The "online now" icon isn't flashing or I'd IM and make fun of him.

I'd wanted to jack off before bed, but now I feel so discouraged I don't even want to think about it. To make things worse, a car just drove by blasting On the Wings of Love's single, "Knit Me a Hat for Winter." I scream "Shut up!" to no one in particular.

I sit up and call the pizza place downstairs — I'm determined to live my life as a shut-in. The guy who does deliveries for them, Juan, brings my two slices upstairs. I tip him a quarter. He knows I'm broke. The apartment is a bit of a giveaway. I take the pizza to my bed to eat, and as I'm chomping, I flip through an *Art Forum* that I've looked through twenty times already. Sherlock left it here a couple months ago. I find the ad for his show, which already closed. It was called "Brooklynism." The ad has one of his paintings of a shirtless boy with electro-clash hair, like, sort of floppy, sitting on a toilet holding a copy of *Boar Hunter* magazine. The sink next to him is filled with blood and there's a hypodermic needle behind him on the tank.

After I'm finished shoving the two slices in my mouth, I fall back in bed. But I can't sleep. My brain has drifted to sex again and now I've got an insta-boner throbbing. I'm beginning to hate my dick. It's always demanding something.

I could go see Pete. He'd probably make out with me, even though he's sort of a sell-out magazine writer. My stomach starts to churn. I feel like the deli poisoned me and my stomach is about to burst open on the rug.

Fuck it. Anything is better than lying here on my bed alone like a loser. I can't stand to be alone for one more second. I pull myself out of bed, throw on a T-shirt, and walk down the hall and knock on Jody's door where Pete is house-sitting. My heart starts beating fast and I feel lame and needy because of it. Why should I care what Pete thinks of me? I know he's there because I can hear the television blasting the laugh track from some stupid sitcom. I consider backing out, running home to my apartment and slamming the door behind me.

Suddenly, the door swings open. Refrigerated air pours out of the room. Holy shit. Air conditioning. The tiny hairs on my forearms stand on end. I can't remember when it wasn't 90 degrees, day or night.

Pete is shirtless, wearing plaid pajama bottoms, the waistband down low, like obvious low, like he pushed them down just for me, barely exposing the top of his pubic hair. My eyes wander up his torso to a leather pouch necklace that looks sort of Navajo, the kind a little boy would wear. His hair is less office-worker than usual, which is a definite improvement. He almost looks cool. He's skinnier than I thought he was, but more muscular, too.

"What's in the pouch?" I ask, not knowing what to say.

He looks embarrassed, like he forgot it was there. "My baby teeth, and my wisdom teeth. That's so weird, isn't it?" He laughs. "I was just looking through my shit — because I brought it over and it's all out — and I found this, so I put it on. I wore it when I was a kid running around the neighborhood doing detective work. My house had no tooth fairy. My mom didn't believe in giving money for fallen teeth." He smiles at me. "What's up?" It's sweet but it makes me feel stupid for some reason.

"I don't know. Sad, I guess."

"Why?" he asks, sounding sort of high and whiny, an emulation of actually caring.

"No friends, no money, no publisher, no gallery, no future, no hope."

"You can't expect all those things if you don't make an effort. Try finishing your book you told me about. Just work for an hour everyday and it'll be finished before you know it. I'd be happy to read it for you if you ever want me to."

"No, I'm too embarrassed to show you anything. You'll think I'm psycho. Besides, you're not exactly my target demographic. Don't you write about, like, abs exercises?" What I'm really thinking is *why would I trust the opinion of a bad magazine writer to analyze my art anyway*?

"I'll still like you." He stretches, both of his arms reaching high for the ceiling, showing off. "Come in."

I want to lean forward and just fall into him, but at the same time, I find Pete so lame that I just want to go home. I guess that's the self-destructive part of me, the part that gave myself a black eye on purpose three times in my life just to gain sympathy from someone who was angry at me. I ignore my instincts and walk inside the ice cold apartment. I don't know how he can stand to walk around shirtless — I'd be freezing cold. I stare at his back — just perfect pale skin — as I follow him over to the couch. I think he might really like me, and for some reason, the thought makes me panic, but it's all buried inside. I doubt he's sensitive enough to pick up on it.

Billy and Sherlock would though. That's the difference between being an artist and not being one — at least one of them, a major one — and possibly the difference between being homo and straight. Straight guys never know what's going on with anyone unless it involves their own dicks.

Pete sits on the green velvet couch.

My stomach churns again. I don't know if I'm panicking or if I'm about to throw up. I have no idea what to say. I think about going into the bathroom, jacking off, shooting the mirror and leaving, but I just blurt out, "Do you wanna make out?" I don't know where this comes from. Desperate loneliness I guess.

"Uh...I don't know," he says so hesitantly I'm sure he's about to tell me he has a disease or that he's straight. "Okay, sure."

As soon as he says he wants to, I'm totally not into it. But he pulls me toward him and he's warm and fuck, I wish I could just escape my own brain for just five fucking minutes. *Five fucking minutes, brain!*

He slides his arms around me and leans in and starts kissing my lips gently. This isn't going to work. I wanted him to kiss me hard and push me into a wall or something. I wanted monkey sex, but his hands are slowly and gently working their way inside my T-shirt and around to my back.

I can't handle this. "Is there any alcohol around or whatever?" I ask.

"Um...." He hesitates. "Yeah, there's some champagne left over from the *Monsieur* party," he says, sounding a little confused. "What's wrong?"

"Dude, I just don't feel it," I say, staring at a frosty bottle of Dom Pérignon in the refrigerator. I can't look at him. I'm such a weirdo freak boy I can't even fool around without fucking it up. I try to change the subject, try to save myself from looking as stupid as I'm acting. "God, this apartment is basically the same as mine, but it seems so much bigger. I guess it's the couch or the TV or the...food."

"And because we actually clean it. That helps."

I'm freaking out inside and I have a throbbing full-on boner. I just want to fuck him; I don't want to have to do this whole stupid ritual of talking to get into it. And I don't want to have to look at him after. He'll probably take a shower and sanitize his body with anti-bacterial soap before and after sex. What does he see in me? If I knew, maybe I could feel better about myself.

Fuck it. I turn around and push my body into his, kissing him hard. I can feel his boner against my leg. I pull down his pants and grab his balls. I drag him down to the floor as we're making out. He starts to suck me off and it feels so fucking good. It's been months. I'm sweating instantly even though it's freezing in here. We jack each other off frantically, coming at the exact same moment. This is the only time I've been out of my head in months. It's such an enormous relief.

He scoots up and cradles my head in his lap. I close my eyes because he looks too sincere and it's obvious he likes me too much and I can't stand it.

I just want to smoke a cigarette and get fucked up

and be alone. I stand up fast and head straight to the unopened champagne. I pop the cork and take a huge drink. I burp.

"What are you doing?" he laughs, lying on his side on the floor. I want to punch him, I really do. He's so not punk. I want to punch myself for making this happen, for giving into this bourgeois bullshit.

I'm embarrassed to be naked in front of him. I'm so fucking pale and skinny. I look like a dirty corpse. Fuck, I don't even know him. I step into my pants and then turn my back to him and pull my shirt on. "I think this was a mistake. I'm sorry. I gotta go." I'm not even lying. I have total post-cum depression.

"What do you mean? Stay. I like you. I know you know that. You don't have a boyfriend. This is just about your insecurity issues, isn't it?"

"No, it's not. You don't *know* me, so don't act like you do. We're just not living in the same world. You're so...I mean, you write for a *men's magazine* and I'm an artist. We're totally different species."

"We're more alike than you think."

"I don't know what I'm saying. I'm sorry. I have to go." I run out, feeling totally stupid, taking the champagne with me to my apartment, which is about 9,000 degrees hotter. I slam the door behind me and close my eyes. *Well, I fucked that up.* I fall back on the bed and take an enormous gulp of champagne. I feel myself getting drunk really fast.

I used to be happy back when I'd just graduated from Cooper Union. I went to openings with Billy all the time and we drank six bottles of the free wine. We made out on subway cars. We took blurry pictures of each other naked. We lived together in a one-bedroom brownstone apartment in Brooklyn. We drank beer on our stoop on warm summer nights. We talked about getting a dog. We said "I love you" when we hung up the telephone. We stole each other art supplies as presents. We listened to punk rock and danced around the apartment in our boxers.

But Billy loved to go out and I sort of hated it. I didn't want to restrict him, make him feel suffocated, so I let him go out alone to openings and after-parties and birthday parties, even once, an underwear party in Brooklyn, although he said he kept his clothes on. At some point while he was going out alone all the time, he met this *textile* artist (*textiles* isn't art, I said, and he got really defensive). He insisted they were just friends. Then after being distant for a whole week straight, he finally said they were in love and he didn't love me anymore because I didn't enjoy anything and how was he supposed to do something positive in life if I was always depressed and dragging him down, blah, blah, blah.

I argued that I was immersed in the novel about a loner I was working on and that in order to have a clear perspective of his world, I sometimes needed to live like a total outsider. Days passed with us barely speaking.

Finally, one night during a thunderstorm that felt like *War of the Worlds* was happening outside our building, Billy said those words. "It's over. I'm moving out." As if to snap me out of shock, a flash of lightning followed by the deepest, loudest crackle of thunder I've ever heard, knocked a wine glass off the windowsill, shattering it on the floor. For a good 30 seconds, I stood there holding my breath staring at the shattered glass on the floor. Talk about a fucking metaphor.

Then he told me about an El Salvadorian skater kid he'd met on the subway. He babbled on but I was only half-listening. I was devastated and jealous, not only because he cheated on me, but because the idea of meeting that skater kid on the subway was romantic and shit like that never happens to me. I cried, then I got sad and whined, begging him not to leave. He tried convincing me that breaking my heart was the best thing for both of us. At the end of the night, the rain was still coming down in sheets.

I heard him get up and get dressed just as the sun was coming out. I laid there motionless just listening to him gathering his keys and jacket, wondering if this was really our last night together. Worse, it turned out to be the last time I'd see him or even speak to him in months.

Of course he came back — I should say snuck in to get his stuff — but only when I was sleeping. I was taking like three sleeping pills a night back then, so he didn't exactly have to be a ninja to get in and out without me noticing. Slowly, over a period of a couple weeks, I'd wake up and find more and more of his clothes and records and art supplies and dishes and books would be gone until there was almost nothing left.

This is when the staying-home-all-the-time thing started. Six weeks was easy. I got to know all the delivery restaurants in the area, I still had cable television and telephone service and some money left from a fund my parents saved to give me when I graduated from college. They weren't thrilled it was art school, but they gave me the money anyway. Anything to keep me in New York and away from them.

I lie down and try to fall asleep, attempting to conjure up a fantasy about doing it with Billy. But every time I get close to him, Pete pops into my head and interrupts and I can't make him go away.

Chapter Three

Always in Between Places

Morning comes. Except for taxis blaring their horns and the forced air sound of buses braking up and down Avenue B, my apartment is quiet — too quiet. It's one of those summer days — hot as an oven even at nine a.m. — but no sunshine, not even clouds really, just a sheet over the city, making my white walls look gray, practically invisible.

I have a piss boner, so I walk over naked to the bathtub in the kitchen and piss into it. (I'd miss the toilet with a hard-on.) Afterward, I don't even rinse the tub. No one's coming over, so who cares if my bathtub smells like dried urine, caked-on spots the color of Lemonheads. My piss smells strong. I'm sure it's because I drink basically no water.

I take a drink of lukewarm water from the tap and I hear Jody dragging her luggage into her apartment. She's back from her business trip I guess.

Pete better not tell her about last night. If he does, I'm sure he'll make me out as a psycho and she'll have one more reason to just give up on me, which I'm pretty sure she's been thinking about doing already.

I plop down on my desk chair. My hand still smells like Pete's dick mixed with spit. I get a little horny smelling it, but that doesn't last long because my stomach aches from being empty and I have no food. I only have about four dollars left until the next unemployment check, which is three days away. That gives me $1.33 a day to eat. Wow, I think, I could eat like what, a bagel? I should have asked Pete for some money before we did it, but I would have looked like a junkie whore, no doubt.

I notice the Metrocard in my wallet. I remember that it has like $60 on it. Maybe I could sell it to someone. I don't really need to ride the subway anyway even though I love to cry on it, just riding around, being taken somewhere, always in between places. That feeling of aimlessness makes everything feel more bearable. But lately, I almost never leave the thirteen-block radius.

I should take a shower because I'm so sweaty, but instead, I just pat an enormous cloud of baby powder on my crotch and pull on a pair of dirty corduroys. I step into my slip-on Vans, splattered with paint from this one painting I made like three years ago — I dumped it on the sidewalk because it was of a fawn and they got too trendy — and grab my keys, which are attached to one of those rubber plastic trolls with neon green hair. I once had a little plastic Beavis, but it's been lost forever.

Billy used to call me Beavis, the memory of which starts this fucking ticking bomb of emotions in my chest. I clench my teeth so I don't start crying as I unbolt all the locks on my apartment door and jump down the three flights and out onto Avenue B. In my doorway, a streamlined looking young Latino dude is selling heroin to a young model-looking girl who's wearing a leopard print tank top and a tiara. I'm so fucking hungry, I realize from smelling food cooking in the deli, so I run down Avenue B toward Houston to the closest subway station.

I hurry down the cruddy stairs past people blocking the steps, finishing their cell phone conversations, and into the urine-scented station. *Is the entire city coated in piss?* The token booth worker, a fat black lady, is asleep in her air-conditioned booth, so I'm not worried about getting caught re-selling my Metrocard. There are signs all over the subway system warning that it's illegal to sell subway cards.

An old man tries to wake her, saying he needs to buy a "senior subway token," which doesn't exist.

I wish I could hit him. Hunger pangs make my stomach feel like it might release the remains of its meager contents of day old pizza onto the floor of the station. *How ironic that the starved throw up more than the fat.* I lean against the wall by the touchscreen Metrocard machines and try to steady myself, try to prevent my body from throwing up. A wave of nausea peaks and starts to die down. The heat doesn't help. Neither does the stench of piss.

A girl who looks sort of like my neighbor, Jody, walks up to recharge her card and says, "You're like green. Are you okay?"

"Yeah," I say, flattered a little by her concern. "Just a little nauseous."

"You should go home then," she snaps. "Don't get the rest of us sick."

"Mind your own business. Fuck," I whine.

"Fuck *you*, asshole."

Wow. How easily people get angry in a heatwave. I steady myself and walk away from her. I want to tell people about my Metrocard being for sale, but I'm too shy to actually say it, so I start to try to explain things to people passing by and they either ignore me, or say, "What?" and then I just turn away or mumble "nothing," like some retard.

Finally after standing there for another twenty minutes, a bald dude with a mustache who looks about fifty walks up to me and somehow deciphers from my pathetic sales job that I want to sell my Metrocard.

"How much?" he asks.

"It's got $60 on it, so I'll sell it for $40, I guess."

"Come with me, sir."

"What?"

He flashes an NYC Transit Police badge from his pocket of his now so obviously undercover cop outfit — ironed jeans and a white button-down shirt. Fuck. "Come with me." I can't believe this is happening. He leads me by the arm through an unmarked metal door beside the ticket booth and down a long hallway of white-painted cinderblock.

He directs me into a covert windowless transit police office. The only good thing is the air-conditioning, which is humming quietly in the corner, competing with the buzz of the fluorescent lights.

"Have a seat, sir." He motions to a folding chair in front of his metal desk. "Re-selling a Metrocard is a violation of *New York City penal law 165.16, selling a*

Metrocard containing value. You're going to get a ticket, your Metrocard will be seized, and you'll be released, unless there's an outstanding warrant. May I see your ID please?" He turns on a computer so ancient I'm surprised it works. The Windows theme from like 1904 plays, triggering a horrible memory of when I caught Billy jacking off on a web cam with his "friend," a skinny nineteen-year-old drug addict with long blond hair and fake professor glasses. I walked up behind him just in time to see the kid shoot all over the front of this thrift store Miami Dolphins T-shirt. Startled, Billy hit restart, triggering that horrible Windows song.

The cop is staring at me like I might be crazy.

(Oh, he's just waiting for my ID and I'm spacing out.) I reach into my wallet and my heart begins to beat really fast, like out-of-control fast. What if this guy knows about my book? What if he knows that I fantasize about pushing? Wait, wait, I tell myself, taking a couple deep breaths. It's just fiction. Besides, there's no way this dude knows what I'm writing about, no way, unless we've got serious big brother going on.

"The ID?" the cop asks again, impatiently.

"Oh yeah." I hand him my New York State ID, which has a photo of me from art school. I had blue hair. The best of times, but I didn't even realize it.

The picture was taken on a crisp fall day. I had a crush on Billy then — I hardly knew him — and Sherlock was just a civilian, pre-art star, when he'd just hang out like a normal person. He actually borrowed money from me that day, like $20.

The cop types some shit into the computer and then his expression changes — he's analyzing something on the screen. He punches a few more buttons and his expression changes from concern to frustration.

"So, anything exciting happen lately?" I ask, as I feel a trickle of sweat roll down my temple.

He ignores my question and says, "I don't know what the problem is here, so what's going to happen is that I'm going to write your desk appearance ticket and you'll be expected to stand in front of a judge on...." He checks his computer screen. "On August twenty-third at 9:30 a.m. If you don't show up, a warrant for failure to appear will be issued. It's in your best interest to show up. I also suggest wearing business casual." He writes *business casual* on the sheet of paper and then asks me to sign the paper to acknowledge that I know about having to appear in front of a judge. He hands me the white copy and tells me I'm finished.

"Uh, actually, can I have just like one swipe-though? I have literally no money and I need to get to Brooklyn," I lie.

He hands me a paper single-use subway card, which I take with another thank you and then leave, walking back out into the stifling piss-scented heat of the subway station. I start to walk outside, back out into the hot, blinding sunny day, but then I think about actually going to Brooklyn with my free ride. I haven't been in almost two years.

The last time was to visit Billy as "friends," at least that was the excuse I gave and the only one he would accept to see me. He was still living in Carroll Gardens with a friend who had just dumped his girlfriend. Billy had just broken up with the textile artist — his boyfriend after me — so they were both all *we just want to be left alone* or whatever, sort of like lesbians. Billy and the textile artist's relationship only lasted two months — two fucking months. For those two months of his happiness and probably lots of sex and making out, he made my life a living hell for almost three years.

So I wait on the platform with the Brooklynites — the skinny indie-rock guitarists and the forty-year-old baby mommies in the unbearable heat, way hotter than the outside temperature for some reason —

you'd think it would be cooler underground — drenched with sweat, for the next F train. I want to see if I can find some piece of Billy in that neighborhood where we used to live.

We lived in Carroll Gardens shortly before every resident of the neighborhood had a twin-sized double baby stroller and a Kate Spade diaper bag. But I secretly loved the place because I felt like the two of us were a family in a family neighborhood. I know that sounds lame, but feeling like a family was something I'd never known before, so it gave me a tranquil joy, it calmed me down. The pace was slower and the streets were leafy and quiet. Billy always wanted to be in the middle of whatever was happening, so he complained about having to live there. I can't even hear the words *Carroll Gardens* without a ball of emotions exploding in my chest, reminding me of the awkward, painful coffee I had with Billy the last time I was in the neighborhood. I'd gone there half-expecting him to tell me he missed me and that he wanted to get back together. I figured if he missed me even one-tenth as much as I missed him, he'd have to want me back. It turns out that was the furthest thing from his mind. He said I was settled and boring. It was then when he told me, "I will never love you again, Kurt. We will never be together again. You have to learn to live with it."

I didn't believe him, even though he acted like he didn't know me anymore at the same time as he acted like he knew me too well to find me interesting. It was true in a way. I was boring because I had no life because I was devastated by his totally dumping me out of the blue. Suicide would have been the most interesting thing I could have mustered back then. The settled part was bullshit. How could I have been settled with $2.12 in the bank and having to sleep on Sherlock's studio floor with no pillow and no heat? After I told Billy that I thought his last boyfriend was lame and how we should have never split up, he scolded me by saying I was overly judgmental about everyone. He knows it's one of my biggest annoyances to be called judgmental, so I know he was just trying to piss me off. I got so mad I burned my tongue on a latte that was so hot it could have triggered nuclear fusion.

Why did I even want this fucker back? I could make myself feel like shit without his help. Besides, he'd let his looks slide. He looked like he'd been drinking too much, or doing too much blow. He'd put on weight and he had dark bags under his eyes.

He even told me he'd met some rich fag who was paying his rent for him. I wanted to throw my latte in his face, but instead, I just bolted from my seat, crying all the way home. By now, half of New York has seen me in tears.

I'd heard from several people including Sherlock that this dude, Justin, who he was living with, was a junkie and kept his nod going by milking his rich aunt. She owned half of Seattle, Billy said.

In going back there to see that apartment, I guess I'm looking for pieces of myself — happiness, confidence, hope — that I lost along the way, where Billy looked at me like I was truly crazy for the first time, where he moved away to after leaving me, where he scoffed at me for suggesting that we might make out before we parted, where he told me point blank that he'd never love me again. I know it's some symbolic gesture that will only make me sad, but I can't help myself. I rarely can.

I take a deep breath to steady myself but inhale the horrible stench of the station — what smells like rotting meat combined with spray paint. It's an instant headache and I know where it's coming from. A hulking yellow garbage train barrels by, an old diesel engine pulling five rusty cars filled with subway trash. After it clears the station, I look up the platform.

A lanky boy walks up behind me, well, not a *boy* really, he's probably around twenty-five like me, but he surely looks healthier and cheerier and more alive than me, but who doesn't? He's wearing the standard black Che Guevara revolutionary cap with tufts of dark brown hair sticking out both sides in front of his ears, and once he gets close enough, I see three woodpeckers tattooed on his forearm — not the Woody Woodpecker cartoon type, but the kind you'd see in a science book. He's listening to an iPod, so everything is probably like a movie to him. New York can be so epic with the right song playing.

This boy is the only good thing that has happened to me all day, a spark of something beautiful in a city that can be hideous and ungraceful, especially in the summer. He's also my excuse for abandoning the stupid ill-conceived idea to go walk around Carroll Gardens to cry and be miserable about Billy. The woodpecker boy waits about ten feet away from me, watching down the tunnel for the train.

Finally, the train pulls into the station and I think about the entire route of the F line, from Coney Island in Brooklyn to 179th Street in Jamaica. I rode the entire stretch one day just for something to do, just to kill an afternoon. If I had friends, I suppose I'd spend days like that sitting in the park or walking around the city.

There's nothing like the feeling I get when riding around on the subways. I just watch the people, eavesdrop on conversations, and imagine the lives of all the different types of people. It's hard for me to believe that other people don't love it, too, though most people complain about riding the subway.

Me and the woodpecker boy walk into the same car. Most of the seats are taken, so we sit down ten feet away from each other.

The conductor announces over the loudspeaker that the train will turn express to Church Avenue in Brooklyn, something that happens sort of often during rush hour, but not usually during the middle of the day. Anyway, what it means is that I'll have to walk twenty blocks in the searing heat to get to a neighborhood that I find totally depressing. Instead of putting myself through that, I jump off the train right before the doors close. To my surprise, the woodpecker boy follows me out.

Our eyes lock for a split-second, both avoiding the wrath of the subway doors as the angry ding signals their closing.

I stand there for a second not knowing whether to try to talk to him or run away, so instead I linger, walking slowly to the nearby subway map. It's encased behind scratched up and acid-graffiti-tagged Plexiglas making it almost impossible to read. I point to where I think my apartment is located and imagine smashing the building.

Meanwhile, like ten feet down the platform, the woodpecker boy is singing, barely, but with some guttural scratchiness in his voice, *"He tells me he swam with sharks last night."* He doesn't mean to be heard, I can tell, and he doesn't realize his voice is above a whisper. When he catches me glancing at him, he looks embarrassed, which I totally love.

It's the first time someone has cared about me looking at them in well over a year. Usually, people — especially young gay dudes — just ignore me.

He looks down the platform for the next train, and I can't tell if he's trying to act casual while waiting for me to go up to him, or if he's hoping I'll just leave him alone. He twirls the wheel on his iPod and I imagine that electronic click that the iPod makes when you spin the white wheel with your finger. He glances my way, catching me staring at him. He must think I'm some stalker.

I look around the station for something to do. Unlike the fancy mosaic murals and baroque columns you see uptown, the metal columns that line this platform aren't ornate even in the slightest way. They're essentially just steel I-beams, painted thick with blue oil paint. There's a plastic sign on each column saying Second Avenue, but some of the blue paint bleeds onto some of the signs, like a lazy subway worker didn't bother to put masking tape on them before painting. It occurs to me that the filthy state of the subway makes me feel at home. My apartment isn't much cleaner.

A rat scurries along the tracks through a mud puddle past a broken cell phone without a battery back, long since abandoned. The sports section of the *New York Times* lies half decomposed in a black sludge near a wad of bright green gum.

It's safe to look at the woodpecker boy again, so I do. We're the only ones waiting for the train on the Brooklyn-bound side. He's gently rocking his head to what appears to be a fast rock song. He glances at me shyly and we sort of lock gazes for about ten seconds.

It's really incredible, just to make contact with another human being — a cool, arty boy with intense eyes and a sexy neck. I think about walking over to him and asking what he's listening to, but I'm a lot too shy to be that forward. And I'm too out of practice socially to pull off any sort of casual, "Hey, what's up?" sort of thing.

Is he walking toward me? Shit.

Instantly, I break out in a sweat, my hands damp, my heart beats faster. What can I say that won't sound lame or crazy?

He comes right up to me all confident and takes out his white earphones, letting them fall across his shoulder. He reminds me of Billy — that sexy, dirty thing — and I'm more excited by him standing right next to me than I've been by anything in years.

I stare down at the tracks, acting like I'm not nervous as fuck that he's standing one foot away from me. Finally, I look up and I'm not sure how my face looks. I can't feel it. I might look like I'm seeing a ghost, telling a lie, trying to piss. I must look scared, because he reacts to my expression by grinning, like he's trying to comfort me or something.

He opens his mouth.

I watch his lips, pointy incisors like fangs.

"Were you the DJ at Smiths night last night?" he asks.

"DJ?"

"Yeah. You were playing all that amazing obscure

stuff, right?"

"No. I hate Morrissey, couldn't have been me." *Why the fuck did I say that?*

"Oh, okay. Sorry." He turns dismissively and watches for the train. He reaches for something in his pocket and a book of matches falls out to the floor. He doesn't notice.

I totally blew it. I stand here feeling inadequate, foolish, meaningless, ugly, undesired, and alone.

He was looking at me like he thought I was cute or amazing or just *worth it* or whatever, and then he totally dismissed me. Now I'm all horny and hapless and I won't do anything else today but obsess about him and what could have been between us. I'll be paralyzed. I thought he was amazing looking, the coolest person in the city just seconds ago, his hazel eyes and messy hair, his T-shirt with a rip in the neck. How could such a perfect person hurt me so bad in just seconds flat? I want to hurt him back. I hear the rumble of the approaching train.

I step behind him and gently grasp his shoulder. I want to push him. I really do. Maybe I want to jump in front of the train with him, killing us both.

He spins around, surprise registering on his face. He's frozen, not sure what to do, like he can't tell if

I'm trying to hit on him or pickpocket him.

Feeling the warmth from his shoulder skin through his T-shirt is an instant boner for me. I know I shouldn't be touching him — he's a total stranger — but I can't help it. "What are you doing?!" he shouts as he pulls away.

Before I can think of an answer, the train glides in, the wind blowing his hair for a few seconds. The doors slide open and he steps into the train, purposely taking a seat facing away from me.

I stand there just staring at the back of his head through the window, unable to move. For a second, I hear no noise, like I'm standing totally alone in an abandoned city. When sound returns, my mouth is dry and I'm dripping with sweat. What the fuck did I just do?

The train pulls out of the station and he's gone. I'm going to punish myself for this by not eating dinner tonight. I won't eat until I pass out. I bend down and pick up the matchbook he dropped. It says Lodge, a restaurant on Grand Street in Williamsburg. Shoving the matches in my pocket, I take off for home.

Chapter Four
Tenement Musk

I walk up the stairs, shielding my face from the inevitable glare of the hot day, still drenched in sweat and shaking. As soon as my eyes adjust to the light, I see a woman pinned under a taxi in the middle of First Avenue, her leg twisted awkwardly beneath her.

A cab driver is pacing around his car, his turban almost falling off. Cars are honking, trying to get around the accident in the clogged intersection.

"Help me!" the lady under the cab screams to no one in particular. Without thinking, I lean down to get a better look at her. Blood is pooling on the street.

A man in a suit screams, "I'm calling 911!" and gets on his cell phone.

I just stand there, frozen, trying not to let myself think of this as a bad omen. My eye is drawn down to the woman's wallet, which is lying on the pavement right at my feet. It must have gotten knocked out of her purse when she was hit by the taxi.

Without thinking, I lean down and snatch it. The leather is cool to the touch.

I tuck it into my armpit and run home.

The sirens from an approaching ambulance echo off the buildings. I run up the stairs to my hot apartment and lock the door behind me. My heart is racing. I don't know if it's from running up the three flights of stairs or that I'm thinking that the police are going to burst in here and arrest me. I sit the wallet on my desk and stare at it in disbelief. I actually stole her wallet. I take a deep breath and open it. I find a driver's license first, 34 Sutton Square, age fifty-four, Elaine Johnston-Rivers, type AB positive blood, organ donor.

A Sutton Square address means she doesn't need the money, but taking the only clue about her blood type sure won't help her at the ER. And I think AB is a rare blood type.

Inside the money compartment there's a gold American Express card, a platinum Visa card, a book of checks. I get to the cash. Five $100 bills and three $20s. It's more money than I've seen since Billy and I counted my money by hand for the lesbian landlady who owned our Brooklyn apartment.

I count the cash again, stick most of it in my desk drawer and $100 of it in my wallet. I hide the credit cards in the bottom drawer of my desk behind all the half-finished novels. I tuck the wallet in my shoe to remind me to find a secret place to throw it away next time I leave the apartment. I pull the woodpecker boy's matchbook out of my pocket and smell it — no remnant of his body, being so close to his leg and his dick left nothing. There's just that slight sulfur scent that all matchbooks have. I carefully prop it up on my bookshelf above my bed on top of *American Daze*, my favorite novel. I try to remember his face, the way his neck had just the slightest hint of blue-blood veins showing on the side. I would jack off thinking of him now, but I'm too hungry, so I try to save images of him for later.

I decide to cancel my self-imposed starvation and go down to the deli and buy a twelve-pack of cold beer and some pretzels, and a couple bottles of San Pellegrino water, because I have to drink more water considering how toxic my piss smells. As I walk back upstairs, I feel like I should feel *something* about stealing a hurt woman's wallet, but I don't. What's worse than not feeling guilty is that I'm happy now because I'm not broke anymore. I go back inside my apartment and open a beer immediately. I sit down at my desk and drink four beers in a row quickly, barely stopping to breathe or piss.

Woodpecker boy gets me thinking about my novel. I lost him, but he can still live forever in my story. I turn on my computer to see if I can pull a couple paragraphs out of my clogged up brain. I start to type.

* * *

Elliot lingered behind a boy while waiting for a train, and he felt like his heart and his lungs and his stomach were floating above him on the subway station platform. He felt that his heart could start bleeding, making the subway platform a sticky red mess. He would be embarrassed if this happened, so alarmed and terrified of his own body he was.

Elliot stared at the boy brutally until the boy noticed. What Elliot didn't know about himself was that he was desired every day on his walks through town. He is delicate and pale, stunningly complex, and men and women both wanted him all the time.

This boy on the subway platform felt the same. He turned his slight body around and stared at Elliot, saying all he could without speaking.

Elliot smiled, just a little, and looked away, to attempt to lead the boy into the maze of emotions that Elliot calls his complicated life. When he desires, he is repelled. He doesn't know why. He thinks of a rat he saw on the Bowery once, determined, direct, scurrying through the filth. He knew what Elliot didn't know, that emotions are useless. Elliot felt he should just attack this kid, rip his shirt off and take him into his arms and kiss him hard until his lips are bleeding. But what he felt he actually could do was push him in front of the next train. He was bitterly cold and his whole being needed to be warmed by this kid who so obviously would go home with him right here and now. But he couldn't. He was much too scared by intimacy to actually go through with it.

He heard a train in the distance, like an earthquake rushing down a faultline. His heart skipped a beat.

The boy takes off his coat. Then, he steps out of his pants and pulls off his T-shirt until he's standing there naked, pale, shivering. It's an alarming sight in the filth of the station, the alabaster of this perfect skinny kid contrasted against the gritty world. He looks even more naked because his body is so simple, so inexperienced.

Elliot just stands there, feeling a buzz take over his dick, like he wants to rip the boy to shreds.

The train glides into the far side of the station.

The angelic naked boy looks up, down, and then to each side. He glances at Elliot, strong and direct.

The train pulls closer, just twenty feet down the platform.

The boy steps gently off the edge of the platform.

Elliot sees the driver pulling the contraptions inside the control booth. The train screeches, halts, twenty tons of metal stopping.

The boy steps gently off the edge of the platform.

Elliot screams, "No! No! No!"

The train conductor's face twists and turns, but he can't stop the train.

It slices this skinny pale boy in half, crimson blood fills the canal between the tracks.

Elliot would never be the same.

* * *

I try to keep going but can't. I'm shaking. And it's like writing drains my body, not only emotionally, but physically. I'm so exhausted that I have to go lie down. Apart from my computer's buzzing blue screen, it's totally dark in my apartment. The door buzzer rings, which scares the shit out of me. It sounds like a fire alarm. I notice my hand is shaking. I'm starving and pretty drunk. I move toward the door, but trip on the bed in the dark.

I look around to make sure the apartment is presentable, whatever the fuck that is. I guess it's okay. I open the door and Sherlock stands there, sweaty and out of breath — he smokes two packs a day and has never lifted more than a paintbrush. He walks in wearing his regular outfit: black skinny jeans, black paint-speckled T-shirt, and his favorite wizard-themed scarf wrapped around his neck like a bandana. He looks around the room, faking total disgust. "It smells like shit in here," he says.

"Yeah, tenement musk it's called. You don't remember it?"

"No man, never heard of it." Sherlock plops down on my bed. "Oh man, all you gotta do is like clean or something."

"Your apartment smelled like this before you got rich, remember? You're smelling poverty."

"How about turning on a light or something."

I switch on the light next to my bed. "Sorry. Do you want a beer?"

"Uh...sure, man."

I reach into the college dorm-sized refrigerator that barely holds a six-pack and hand him a beer.

"So what'd you do last night?" I ask.

"DJed Brit-pop night. And then? Oh yeah. I took some unidentified flying pill and passed out behind the bar. I woke up at Billy's house next to some wired SVA student."

"You woke up at Billy's house?"

"Yeah, why?" he asks nonchalantly like he doesn't know that he's hit an all-time major nerve with me.

"Does he have a boyfriend, I mean, does Billy?"

"I think that was my job, at least last night."

"What do you mean?!" I can't even look at Sherlock right now. He's so pissing me off. He had a threesome with Billy. Could it be any worse? Not possibly.

"I'm joking, Kurt. I slept on the couch as far as I know. This sculptor dude and me slept feet to head, you know what I mean, like on the same couch. He was naked though. Maybe I kicked him in the balls all night long. I really can't remember. It was fucking hot. I remember that. Billy's air conditioner blows out like luke-cool air or whatever it's called."

"So you didn't see the new boyfriend?" I take another beer from the fridge and take a deep gulp.

"They broke up or some shit. I knew the kid. I did a painting of him like a couple months ago. He was Billy's typical type. He looked a lot like you, but like . . . younger, and he had more of a, I don't know, a *scowl* on his face. The painting sold to some Chelsea fag who listens to Coldplay like a month ago. I had to go over to his apartment to *recommend* where to hang the thing. I was like, *how about nowhere*? How about you stop the fucking *Coldplay* so I can fucking think without this sissy boy Gwyneth Paltrow bitch screaming in my ears? He ended up hanging it in his fucking weight room." Sherlock takes his first sip of beer and makes a face that says he doesn't like it. "This beer is sick, and warm."

"Sorry, my refrigerator doesn't really work. And it rejects PBR."

"You should invest in a cooler. They have these Styrofoam ones in the delis that are like $1.99."

I can't really think right now. The thought of Billy and *any* other boy makes me want to buy a dagger and systematically go through Williamsburg and pierce each of his little sluts' craniums.

"Listen Kurt, I need to talk to you about something."

I sit down on my desk chair and swivel around to face him, sure this conversation is going to be about not lending me money anymore, and how I have to get over Billy and start leaving my apartment more, and how can I ever find a new boyfriend if I don't take baths or comb my hair or blah, blah, blah. "Don't tell me I need to get out more. I was just out today. I picked up this beer with my own hands; it's not delivery. And it was fucking hot outside. I'm still sweating."

He looks serious. He didn't laugh at my *elitist wimpism*, as he calls it. "Okay. I'm just going to say it. A friend we went to Cooper Union with called me yesterday asking about you. You remember Daniel? He was the one who made the yarn sculptures?"

"Uh...yeah. I hated — hate — him...those. They were so, what's the word, pathetic or something. They jumpstarted my Darwinistic impulse to kill."

"Yeah, I agree, but that's not what I was talking about. He said he saw you at the Second Avenue subway station the other day and he said it looked like you were about to push this kid he knows. This dude, his name is Sammy I think, told Daniel that he thought you might have been actually going to push him, so...you know, he was like, *concerned*."

I feel totally exposed. Why does every arty homo in the city have to know each other? It's incestuous and sick. I can't believe I didn't notice that asshole.

I stare at the woodpecker boy's matchbook leaning against *American Daze*. I feel like it's going to spontaneously ignite, maybe fly toward me and set my hair on fire.

"Yeah, I'm sure, *concerned*. He's a liar. He hates me. I was just, like, *talking* to that dude. I think he liked me. I'm sure Daniel's just jealous."

"Well he told Daniel you were talking to him and then you got all weird and put your hand on his shoulder like you were going to shove him just as the train pulled in. That sounds pretty fucking weird."

"What the fuck? I don't know." I take another big sip. "Everyone's paranoid in this city." I almost choke on my beer, and I end up coughing so much it hurts.

"Are you okay? Do you need, like the Heimlich maneuver or something?"

I manage to stop choking and nod that I'm okay.

"Why don't you talk to me about shit, Kurt? If some dude likes you, you should tell your friends. We used to talk about shit like this. Until you became obsessed with Billy. You know, it's way past time you got over that whole thing. It's never going to happen. Billy's just, I don't know, fucked up, way more fucked up than even you." He fiddles with his scarf, wrapping it around his head like a babushka and looking around my apartment like he's hunting for clues. What does he expect to find, a rotting mangled corpse? "Do you need to talk about anything?

'Cause you know I love you right? You're my, like, friend or whatever. You know that, right?"

"Yeah, I know, Sherlock." That was so convincing, too. "Did you know I'm two months behind on rent? Harold totally wants to rent out the apartment to someone else, probably some just-graduated Oberlin creative writing student with a trust fund, that fucking asshole, or some yuppie spawn." I look down at my hands. They look scuffed and old. "I miss you, man. I hardly ever see you anymore."

"Bullshit. I'm here right now," he says defensively.

"Yeah, but not *really*. It's like we're different species now. Why don't we ever just hang out and get stoned and laugh like we used to? Remember when we'd just randomly pick different streets and go in every restaurant and every store on the street? That was so fun."

"I'm busy now. I'm trying to become a legend, man. I work hard."

"Yeah. I know." I'll never be a legend, that's for sure.

My alarm clock goes off, making both of us practically jump out of our sweaty skins. I reach over and switch it off.

"Fuck, that was unnecessary." He takes a couple deep breaths.

"Look man, don't worry about me. It's all one big mistake. Yes, I'm crazy, but I'm not like *that*."

"You know," he says all serious, "I have a reputation now, and rich people buy my work. I can't afford to get caught up in anything stupid. I'm not even buying drugs myself these days, I pay someone to do it for me. Are you *sure* there's nothing I should know? I mean, I realize you're depressed, man, but don't start blaming it on other people or whatever." He reaches into his pocket, maybe looking for his keys.

"Okay, Sherlock. You can trust me. God, you sound like my mom. Lighten up. It's *me*."

He stands up and takes out his wallet. "How much is the rent on this shithole?"

"$710 a month. You're not leaving, are you?"

"I have to get going. Who should I write the check to?"

"Harold."

He leans over my desk and writes a check for $1,420 to Harold, my landlord, and hands it to me.

"Thanks, man. You're a true friend. And you carry checks with you. That's totally rad and old school."

"See you later, dude. Oh, you should check out the new *Vogue Homme*. There's an article about me in it."

He leaves without a hug, a smile, or even a wink, not that Sherlock has ever been the winking type.

I have a feeling he won't be back for a long, long time. I close the door behind him and practically collapse like a folding chair.

What did that asshole see, that stupid yarn artist? Where was he? Hiding behind a pole or something, that sneaky fuck.

I lie down on my bed and pull the sheet up over my head. I feel so ashamed. I'll close my eyes and when I open them again, it'll be different. There won't be any stupid untalented artists narcing on me to my only friend, and Billy will be sitting at my desk writing lyrics and I'll be snuggled up on the couch inside our old brownstone apartment in Carroll Gardens and all this will be behind me.

Chapter Five

The Harder
It Rained,
the More
We Loved It

I open my eyes. It's raining. Big, almost tropical drops pour from the sky. The thunderstorm makes me feel just a miniscule bit better, but only because it makes me feel less significant. Storms always make things seem less important. Maybe I should live somewhere where it rains constantly, like Seattle. I find comfort in the corners of what others don't like. I like knowing that I have refuge in situations others hate. I can be happy on a cold and rainy day because I feel like everyone else is wishing it would get warmer and drier. That leaves me space to be me. It's hard to explain, but it's comforting, like sad music.

I get up and drink two more beers to stop myself from obsessing over everything. It feels like the room is cooling down a little, too, which is rare. It must be the downpour.

My head is itchy, so I decide to take a bath. I haven't taken one in like five days. I pull off my T-shirt, smelling my armpits as I do, then slide off my pants and boxers. I've got goosebumps. It's like I'm coming off heroin, but I'm not.

Sometimes the only cure for this feeling is cool water. My bathtub has been my ocean and my swimming pool this summer. It's the perfect size for just one person. I step into the three inches of cool water, then slowly lie back. Once the water gets deep enough, I turn it off with my feet. The bathtub becomes stained, a barely perceptible tan just from the dirt that was caked on my body. A flash of lightning crackles and I worry for a second about getting electrocuted. *Unknown Twenty-Five-Year-Old Artist Electrocuted in Bathtub During Lightning Storm.* How boring I would seem. How lonely. Maybe that's cool, though, I can't decide.

I slide down to let my head go underwater for a second and then back up, water streaming onto my shoulders.

I wonder why that asshole would want Sherlock to think I was about to push someone in front of a subway even if it were true. It's not like I'm a threat to him, his fucking *yarn fame*, his stupid *career*. Maybe it's because I saw him at the park a couple months ago and his boyfriend was totally eyeing me. Maybe it's jealousy. I wish all the gay boys in New York City would just fuck each other and get it over with.

Thunder booms, shaking my building, so I decide to get out of the water just in case. I walk across the room dripping to find a towel, but they're all shoved in some nasty ball in the corner. I used them last week to clean up an entire carton of spilled milk, but didn't bother to hang them up to dry. So I grab a bunch of paper towels and dab dry my entire body. I need to get out, and I like walking around in the rain because it keeps the friendly, cheerful people away. I have to break this horrible rut.

I pull on a black T-shirt and head outside, my head cool from my hair still being wet. Then I remember the check Sherlock gave me. I grab it from my pocket, kiss it, and slide the check into Harold's mail slot, relieved at least that I don't run the risk of being homeless, at least for another thirty days.

I walk fast down Avenue B and around the corner on 7th Street. As expected, the rain has driven almost everyone from the street and I feel sort of free for the first time in days. That is until I walk past a record store with On the Wings of Love's album cover art in their window. It's a shot of the whole band — Billy and three other dudes — shirtless in the woods, sitting amongst some tall grasses. Billy loves rainy days, too. When it was gloomy outside, we sometimes stayed in bed all day listening to music and watching the radar on the weather channel's website for especially heavy downpours. The harder it rained, the more we loved it.

I duck into a deli cum magazine shop to check out the new art magazines. There's an ad for Sherlock's next show in *Art Forum*. This reminds me to check out the *Vogue Hommes* article he told me about, which has a photo of him jumping on a bed. Fuck. That must be in his new apartment, which I haven't even seen. How lame that I'm seeing it for the first time in fucking *Vogue*. I haven't really hung out with *anyone* in almost a year. Is it me or is it the world that's keeping me away from everyone?

Suddenly, I spot the dramatic headline of the *Post*. The headline is huge and bold: *TEENAGER PUSHED IN FRONT OF SUBWAY TRAIN*. My heart crashes to the floor of the deli. Am I imagining this? I pick up the paper and go straight to the article. It tells how a seventeen-year-old skateboarder was pushed at the Delancey Street station last night. There are no witnesses except for the F train's operator, who said he saw a dark-haired young man push the victim, then run away. The boy was a Stuyvesant High School student and was a sponsored amateur skateboarder. His name is Jared McClaren. There he is in a black-and-white photo. His floppy dark hair hides one eye, making him look sort of conniving, and the other eye looks totally intense, like crazy alive. You can tell even though the photograph is shitty quality.

Fucking hell. This concept used to be so sexy and mysterious until now. Now, it scares the shit out of me. It's as if my book has come to life. My character, *Elliot Collinsworth*, has actually pushed someone and it's the creepiest coincidence ever. A siren echoes nearby. Maybe they tracked me down and they're racing their big American sedans to this deli right now, but what the fuck could they arrest me for? I'm totally innocent, but I can't help wonder if somehow I did it. Like maybe there's a part of my brain that I don't know about that's controlling the rest of me. As if the Elliot Collinsworth part of my brain dragged me out of bed last night and made me push that kid without even remembering it. I know that this couldn't have happened, but there is this annoying hard-to-shake glimmer of suspicion that I'm somehow involved.

I give the deli owner a quarter for the paper and then take off running back to my apartment in the pouring rain. I'm drenched. I unlock my door and once inside, fall immediately against the bed. I squeeze my eyes shut and try to force myself to black out, but my aching stomach won't let me. So, I turn on my computer and highlight the entire *Push* document, seventy-eight pages, and hit delete. Elliot Collinsworth is gone with the push of a button. The white blank page is all that remains, the cursor blinking, waiting — for me. Sadness starts to swell in my chest, almost the same feeling as when Billy said he was moving out. The same sadness as when my childhood dog, Arrow, died soon after having puppies on the tile floor of the laundry room.

I select *undo delete* and Elliot is back, his thrilling life and miserable failures all laid out in perfect Courier type. He'll live on for now because I let him. I lean back in my chair, spotting the woodpecker boy's matchbook on the shelf. I try to remember what he looked like, and I almost reconstruct his face in my imagination.

I decide to go out to the bar he asked me about. Maybe he'll be there and I'll convince him that he was completely wrong about me, that what he told Daniel about me almost pushing him was all in his head. I'll actually *try* to make some friends, at least to find a dude to make out with. I blow myself a kiss in the mirror and hold my arms up behind me head. My armpits smell sort of great, like animal, like another boy, or sort of like a campfire. The bar he was talking about is really close to my apartment, just down off Avenue A, only like six blocks away. That's one thing so fucking weird about New York. You can be inside your own tiny freak-world apartment surrounded by your things — basically unaware of anything outdoors except for passing fire trucks — and then you walk outside and there's this whole huge universe of people you don't, nor will ever, know, and they're all, or at least most of them, completely in their own worlds. It can be either totally profound or devastatingly lonely, depending on what kind of mood you're in.

I cut over on 8th Street to Avenue A toward the bar. The rain is just a drizzle now and the heat and humidity are on the rise. From a half-block away, I can tell which bar it is, the one with loads of people outside of it smoking and talking. It seems like it's only the art students who still smoke. Three loud, messy-haired girls sit on the wet sidewalk in the drizzle, smoking brown cigarettes, all wearing turquoise pumps and black leggings.

I take a deep breath, then two more, which is what it takes to keep me moving forward. It would be so easy to just turn back and crawl into bed. I force myself to keep going forward. I channel Elliot. He's brave. He'd never turn around and hide.

I walk inside the bar, what is possibly the hottest room on earth, so hot that even the black walls look like they're sweating. I scan the room for Billy or Sherlock, the first thing I always do in any crowded room where they could possibly be. I don't see either of them. They're probably doing shots together. I'm sure there's some sexy dude in his underwear, wearing something like a marching band hat, but only as a joke, in the vicinity. And he has a crush on one of them, most likely Billy.

I notice the back of some boy's head that looks sort of familiar. Walking around to his side, I try to see if I recognize him without him noticing me looking. As I come up behind a couple of Asian dudes in fedoras, I see his face. It's the woodpecker boy. I'm not sure why, but it's scary for me to see him here so suddenly, like a fucked up part of my brain went ahead and pushed him into the train. I hadn't expected to feel like this — all I wanted was a chance to see him again. I hide from him, walking fast toward the small back patio where people are hanging out in tight circles smoking cigarettes. As soon as I walk down the two wooden steps onto the postage-stamp-sized patio, I know it's a mistake. Daniel, the yarn artist, the asshole who claims he saw me almost push the woodpecker boy, is holding court over some younger twink artist boys with hair in their eyes. I want to turn inside out. I consider bailing, but before I can, Daniel spots me and waves, a smug, condescending expression on his face that only a gallery-represented artist standing in front of stupid admirers could manage. He walks toward me, closing in on me, rudely bumping into people on his way across the crowded patio.

I panic over this guy, which makes me feel even stupider than I normally feel.

If he forces me to talk about that day, I'll come off sounding like a liar and he'll call Sherlock. Instinctually, I flip him off and then duck inside, headed straight for the door.

I run around the corner, out of breath, and hide behind a stinking dumpster for a few minutes waiting for him to come outside to try to find me. But he never does, which is actually sort of depressing in a weird way.

I need a thrill, which is the understatement of the year. My "evening out" was a catastrophe. I walk to Tompkins Square Park to score some cocaine. I need a thrill. I buy a $40 bag from a big muscular guy and rush home. I snort the whole bag, in spite of the fact that it tastes and feels like jet fuel. In about an hour, I decide to reorganize my bookshelves. But by the time I've taken them all down, I'm too tired and wired at the same time to put half the books back up. So I go to bed finally with half the books stacked in massive skyscrapers surrounding my bed.

Chapter Six

Scared of Myself

I'm on a ship that's blowing its horn because the water is churning violently and the captain thinks we might not make it. I only know this because of gossip from the other passengers, which happen to include Billy and his stupid textile artist ex-boyfriend. Daniel is the captain.

The ship blasts its horn again and I realize this is not a dream, it's someone at my door pressing the buzzer. I jump out of bed in a cold sweat, headache pounding from the bad coke and the six or seven beers I drank while snorting it.

It's the cops! Who else would it be?

Daniel tipped them off. I'm going to jail. Life is over. I'll never finish a novel. I'll never have another boyfriend. I'll never jerk off in peace again. I'll be raped by hairy murderers with teardrop tattoos. I'll be some old con man's bitch, his Maytag. I'm going to have to kill myself. There's no other way out.

I throw on my terrycloth robe and run down the

three flights of stairs to see who's outside buzzing. At least the outside door was locked for once.

I peek through the bulletproof window in the steel door and see an ironically unstylish baseball cap that says Vail in a 1970s-looking font. I'm safe. No self-respecting cop would wear this hat. I open the door and lo and fucking behold, it's *Billy*!

A warm glow swells in my chest. I know my life will be okay. I won't be arrested. I won't push anyone into subway trains. I'll finish my novel and sell it for like $50,000 and be a literary sensation.

Billy kicks the shit out of my little fantasy right away, of course. "What happened to you?" he asks, all huffy.

"What do you mean?"

"You look terrible."

"I was out late," I lie.

"Why did you call me last night?"

"I *didn't* call you. I came home and passed out. I didn't call anyone."

"What? Then you're too stoned to remember. Ryan was over and he said you blathered on and on and on about how you needed me and how the *ship's captain* was telling us we'd better have sex now before the *ship sinks*. What the *fuck*, man? What are you on?

Ryan thinks I'm fucking around with you now and he's pissed. Explain, asshole."

"I don't know what the fuck you're talking about Billy. Come inside. *Who's Ryan*? The *textile* artist? I thought you broke up."

He stands there for a second on the sidewalk obviously not wanting to come inside my building. I feel like I'm the biggest loser on earth and he feels like it might rub off on him. "Listen." He barely steps inside. "I'm only here because I'm running an errand nearby and I wanted to tell you face to face that you've got to stop all this obsessive shit. You can't keep it up. We're over. And your breath smells horrible."

"Sorry, I just woke up."

He follows me up the stairs. "Incidentally, we did break up. We're back together . . . sort of. I like some-one else. This dude who's currently homeless. And a girl. I'm not going to tell you about them, though, so don't ask."

"I won't. Believe me, I don't want to know."

He follows me into the apartment, my clothes from last night twisted and scattered on the floor, my desk a mess of beer bottles, a CD case with a rolled up $20 bill on it, open journals, mostly about him,

"I can't believe you're still living like this." He takes off his hat and throws it on my bed, which is like bad luck or whatever, so I throw it on the chair.

"It looks like an emo bomb went off in here."

"Ha. Good one," I say sarcastically.

He sits down on my bed and I plop down right next to him, like way too close for his comfort, because he immediately moves away from me. "You know, Kurt. It's been a year since we broke up. We've talked about this a million times. We're just too alike to be together. We don't get along because of it."

"We could. I love you, Billy. I miss you so much," I say, looking down at my lap. "I really miss you. I feel like we've grown enough that we could really make it work now." I can't look up at him because I'm afraid he's going to get mad at me.

"I miss you, too, Kurt. I was so in love with you, dude. I never felt connected with anyone else as much as I did with you."

I'm so shocked to hear this.

Then he continues. "But we're not together anymore. It didn't work out. We tried hard. You know that. Don't make it hard for me to hang out with you by always doing this. I want to be able to be friends and I can't deal with you if every time we hang out, you start harping on this shit." He puts his arm around me and shakes me. "Come on, dude. You gotta reach out and get what you want. You'll find someone else."

I lean over and start kissing him, on the lips, with tongue.

He clamps his mouth shut and stands up, pulling away from me. "You stink, man." He knocks over a tower of books as he moves away.

I have an instant boner. I want him to know I do, but I'm afraid he'll leave if I tell him, so I don't.

He sits down at a safe distance on my desk. "See, that's exactly what I mean."

"I'm sorry." I'm so not sorry. I'd do it again right now if I could. "I feel so strongly for you."

"If you're going to lie about not calling me last night, I guess if there's nothing to talk about besides us getting back together, I'll just leave."

"Wait. I really *don't* remember calling. I did have a dream you were in, with *Ryan* on a ship. It's stupid but we were sailing through rough waters and I was scared and I was like, *needing you to comfort me or whatever.*" I bound over to Billy and kiss him again.

"Stop! Off limits, dude," he shouts. But I don't stop.

And he sort of kisses back, soft, with tongue, wet, deep.

I reach down his pants and he moans a little, light and guttural. He doesn't realize it though. He talks even though I'm clamped onto his mouth. "Daniel said you ran away from him last night at Lit," he mumbles.

"I did not. I was...just leaving," I mumble back. I start stroking his dick, which is now half hard.

"Stop!" He stands up, pulls away from me, and walks over to my mini-fridge for a beer. He doesn't say anything for a good thirty seconds. "Wow, you actually have beer. That's a first. Where'd you get the money to buy beer?"

"I stole it from a lady who got hit by a car."

"Yeah right. Sherlock loaned it to you. He told me he was just over here last night. He asked me to stop by to check on you. He said you looked and smelled like shit. He said you looked crazy."

"So that's why you're here? Because Sherlock told you to?"

"No, I didn't mean it that way. I wanted to see you. I miss you, too. It's like you think I'm a robot and I don't have any emotions. We had something great. But it didn't work out. We just weren't compatible. But you're never going to get over it if you just sit in this shitty apartment all the time. Fucking *do* something, man. You're gonna wake up an old man and be like, *fuck, I wasted my whole life complaining about everything, but I never actually did anything myself.*"

I just sit there like I've been punched in the forehead, knowing that what he's telling me is true. Like I haven't thought about it a billion times. "It's hard for me. I don't *have* any fucking friends. You have like 10,000."

"That's because I actually make an effort. I don't just sit at home whining about how pathetic my life is, how I'm so lonely and I'll never make a name for myself. I know you don't like my band, but at least we're doing it. We're putting ourselves out there and you know what, we're fucking hitting. People love us. That will never happen lying in bed feeling sorry for yourself." He looks at me expectantly, like his words were supposed to inspire me to get up right now and finish my novel. Instead, I just stare at the floor feeling stupid.

He stands up. "I gotta take off. Don't call me in the middle of the night, please. Okay?" He stands by the door.

I stand up. "Why'd you even come over if you weren't going to stay?"

"Kurt, you've got to stop making it a pain in the ass for people to hang out with you. You've got to pull it together. See you later." He turns and heads down the stairs.

I close my door quietly and walk back to my bed and sit in the warm place where Billy's ass just was. I turn on my old AIWA portable radio to the local NPR station, WNYC. The weather guy says that the heatwave is only going to get worse, possibly up to 105 degrees, 115 with humidity by tomorrow or the day after, which would be an all-time high temperature for New York City ever. The weather seems to be conspiring against me. Maybe it will get hotter and hotter until the city finally melts off the face of the earth.

I lean out the window for some fresh air and notice a skinny Mick Jagger-looking kid with a guitar pass right by Billy on his way out. This dude is even walking like Mick Jagger — a boyish but feminine swagger like he knows he's sexy and he doesn't care if you think so or not.

As if this kid is an omen, I leap across the room and take off down the stairs. I have no idea why —

maybe it's Billy walking out on me again — but I have to be near this boy. I have to see him up close. It's an instant crush, my least and most favorite of all human emotions, the emotion that makes you worship someone you don't know.

When I get outside, he's only a half-block up buying some cigarettes from the coffee shed where the goth kid sells lemonaid in the summer and espresso in the winter.

I run up from behind and follow him into a bar called Mamas. He waves to the bartender, who looks like a Norwegian alterna-singer boy. The Mick Jagger kid gives him a couple of CD-Rs with stuff drawn on them with a black Sharpie.

Neither of them notices me lingering by the jukebox, trying to hear every word.

After a short chat, the Mick kid gives the bartender a high five (potentially lame, but still in the realm of cool in his case) then struts outside, his posture purposely rooster-esque.

I chase him down Avenue B, then left on First Street and up First Avenue toward the L train station, which is where I guess he's headed to. I was right. He steps down into the L train platform.

I wait for him, getting a good look at him as he recharges his Metrocard at the vending machine. He's really cute in a British invasion way. His eyes almost sparkle, even at a distance.

When he's finished, I follow him down the stairs to the Brooklyn platform. He still hasn't spotted me. I stand close enough to him to stare at the back of his neck. I get a boner just thinking about seeing him shirtless. I scan every possible surface of his arms, small blond hairs on his forearms, a small scab from a cut on his wrist.

He takes a book out of his bag and sits down on a bench, his guitar leaning on his knee. The book's jacket says it's about the history of opium — white with an orange poppy on the cover.

I hear the train finally coming, the gentle rumble which quickly turns into an almost unbearably loud roar as it reaches the station, pushing stale air before it through the tunnel.

The subway door opens and we're blasted by the cold air inside, a relief to say the least. He takes a seat by the door and I sit directly across from him.

His legs are open wide, his book propped on one knee, with the guitar on the seat next to him. He doesn't seem to notice or care that I'm staring at him as the train starts to move.

We pass through Bedford and right before the Lorimer stop, he takes a deep breath, stands up, and grabs his guitar.

I stand up too, trying not to appear too conspicuous.

We both get off, me trailing just feet behind him.

A kid who looks and sounds like the angsty indie-boy-star Conor Oberst from Bright Eyes only blonder is playing guitar in this inferno of a station, his velvet-lined case opened wide on the filthy cement floor with a few dollar bills and some coins inside.

Young Mick stops for a second to watch him, grinning. When the song is over, they hug, which makes me cringe. Fuck.

I pass by them, slow as possible, then hide behind a metal column. My heart is thumping, I realize, and sweat is dripping down the sides of my torso.

A minute later, the guitar kid plays a Nirvana riff — *Smells like Teen Spirit* — and they both laugh, hug again, and young Mick walks toward the G train platform, taking his iPod from his pocket and putting in the earphones.

I follow him. This is Billy's subway station, I realize, the intersection of the L and G trains. He must walk these routes every day, sometimes two or three times. I imagine him striding down the corridor, a friend on each arm, people gossiping about being at his show the previous night, texting about how they think he's hot.

I follow young Mick through the passageway from the L to the G line platform, not caring if he notices me now. This has to come to something. I can't keep following people forever.

When we get to the platform, there aren't many people waiting for the G train, probably because it's mid-afternoon. A couple of other people wait on the other side of the platform, but only one other person stands on our side — an Asian girl listening to a turquoise off-brand MP3 player, an obvious ballet dancer because she's practicing slightly combinations dancing as she waits.

I want to go up to young Mick so bad. Why can't I just walk up to him and say, "Hey" or whatever? Why does everything have to be so stressful and impossible for me? I take a couple steps toward him, deciding that I *must* do something, even if I just feel him up like some pervert. He's totally controlling me, although he doesn't know it. I follow every tiny clue he gives me. Why can't be just notice me? Am I that invisible? Am I that undesirable? I stare at the back of his head, trying to send him a telepathic message to turn around and look at me. I focus on him so hard that my eyes go blurry. Beyond him, I notice someone familiar. Holy shit. Across the tracks, Billy comes floppily down the stairs, carrying his stupid messenger bag that the textile artist made for him. He doesn't yet see me, so I duck behind the column, still within feet of young Mick.

Mick's making me crazy. I want him so bad. If he doesn't want me, why can't he just let me go? I really want to push him. I can't think about anything else. Not even Billy, other than I hope he's watching me. I want him to see how serious I can be, how I can influence fate all by myself, that I'm no longer some paralyzed loser sitting home alone.

As the shiny aluminum train glides into the station, something in my brain clicks.

I creep up behind young Mick. He's lost in his iPod, not suspecting a thing.

Billy comes to a standstill, spotting me across the tracks. He's staring at me like he's trying to figure out the next fucking crazy stunt I'm going to pull.

Fuck him. Fuck me. Fuck Mick, especially him. He's asking to be pushed, daring me, really convinced he's so out of reach.

Standing squarely behind him, and with more force than I thought I had, I push Mick into the side of the speeding train. His body bounces off the side and he's thrown back onto the platform like a puppet. He looks so fragile, not even making a noise, not crying or screaming, just lying there, his lip and nose bleeding and I assume, totally freaked out.

I just stand here, frozen, for what seems like a thousand hours.

More than hurt, Mick looks stunned, totally shocked. He tries to stand, but halfway up he falls down. His guitar is lying at an angle, still in its case, its neck pointing at me accusingly.

Billy is as still as a tree, obviously stunned, too. Suddenly, he screams my name, which echoes through the station. Hearing my name makes the seriousness of the situation apparent.

I just really fucked up.

The train clears the station. I bolt for the stairs after one last glance at Billy. He's blurry. I might be crying; I can't tell. I'm nauseous and thrilled at the same time. Billy is frozen, standing there, stiller than a tree, watching, silent. He's staring at me hard, even from a distance of twenty yards. Taking three steps at a time, I dodge an MTA guy on his way down. I reach the top of the stairs and dive into a health food store.

In no time, a police car squeals to a stop right in front of the subway entrance. A policeman leaps out, leaving the door open and the lights flashing.

I take off down Metropolitan, running ten blocks until I'm out of breath. My adrenaline rush is the only thing that's keeping me from passing out. I flag down a gypsy cab on Union and two minutes later, I'm on the bridge to Manhattan. The driver drops me off on my corner, I pay him the $20 and run up to my apartment, bolting all the locks behind me, as if *I* wasn't the dangerous one.

What have I done? I fucking *snapped*. I so totally lost it that I'm sort of scared of myself.

My phone rings. Fuck. It has to be Billy. I check the caller ID and it's his cell phone. I can't answer. I have no idea what to say.

I listen to his message as he leaves it. "What the fuck, Kurt?! What did you just do? I hope you're at the police station right now, because if you aren't, I'm telling them. Call me back."

Fuck. I can't breathe. I'm going to pass out. I watch out the window for three hours, until it gets dark, for cops to show up, but they never do.

Someone has opened a fire hydrant for kids to play in, a classic New York image that makes everything seem suddenly so uncomplicated, like me pushing Mick happened a lifetime ago.

Instead of just sitting here letting my paranoid thoughts totally freak me out, I decide to go downstairs to the place where young Mick talked to the bartender earlier today to try to fish around for some information about him. I figure it's safe since no one but Billy saw me do it. Besides, I feel genuinely horrible for hurting him. I almost feel like it wasn't me who pushed him.

I hurry downstairs to the bar, take a seat on the closest bar stool, and order a beer, trying to sound normal. The bartender knows young Mick and I feel like I have to find out if he's okay. I motion him to come over. "Another beer?" he asks.

"Sure," I say, then I just come out with it in one big gulp of a sentence. "I saw this guy here earlier and I think I used to know him. He looks a little like...*Mick Jagger*?"

The bartender laughs. "Yeah, he wishes. So you know him?"

"What's his name? I think he might be this dude I knew back in college."

"Mick," he says, laughing. "No, it's Robin McNally."

"Robin?"

"Do you know him?"

"Uh, no, actually it wasn't him after all. The guy I'm thinking of was named Sam something."

"I'm supposed to see Robin tonight actually. He's gonna come by the bar and spin." He motions to a record player set up back behind the far side of the bar. "He's got a demo that he just finished recording, so I said he could play it."

What's his band called?" I drop a $20 on the bar and stand up.

"It's just him. Robin McNally. He's really good, you should come by for the demo."

"Cool."

"Yeah, man. Later." He grabs his rag and wipes the spot where I was leaning on the bar like he's trying to get rid of any of my lingering spirit, dead skin cells or whatever...any DNA. It's intense.

I have to piss pretty bad, but I decide to hold it till I get home. I round the corner to find Sherlock hovering outside my building with a look on his face like he's my father and I've just totaled his brand new Mercedes-Benz.

"What?" I ask, anticipating the biggest lecture of all time.

"Let's go inside fast," he whispers. I key in and open the door and he slinks in behind me. He pushes me up the stairs and into my apartment. He shoves me inside.

"What the fuck man? Don't fucking push me!" I immediately push him back way harder than he pushed me.

He tumbles back into the kitchen counter, but catches himself. "Fuck! I'm *sorry*. Jesus fucking *Christ*, man. Lay off. I'm here to help."

"I have this thing about being pushed," I say quietly. I walk over to the toilet to piss. "Sorry."

"Obviously, dude." He looks around my apartment like he's about to say something important but can't find the right words. Finally, he says, "Look, Billy told me what you did in the subway."

As soon as he says *subway*, my heart skips two beats. I have to lie. Fast. There's no way he'll understand why I did what I did. Even *I'm* not exactly sure. I'll never be able to explain it. "What'd he say?" I finish pissing, turning around and zipping up my pants.

Sherlock won't even look me in the eye, so he must know the whole fucked up story. "Billy said it looked like you pushed some kid into a train? I don't know *what* the fuck to think. At first, I thought he was super stoned or that he was, like, talking metaphorically about your fucked up relationship. But he's really convinced it was you and he's flipping out over it. He told me about that other kid that was pushed, the one in the *Post*."

"I don't even take the subway anymore," I say, a flat denial, a totally stupid uncreative one at that. "I haven't left this apartment in like *weeks*."

"Billy said he saw you, man. Anyway, you were just outside, so don't give me that shit about never leaving your apartment."

"You're right. I think Billy *was* stoned. He accused me of calling him the other night, too, and I didn't do that either. And think about it: how many dudes look just like me in this city? I must have like . . . twenty-five *doppelgangers*, and that's just on the L train line."

He takes a deep breath, then slumps down in the chair and looks at me like I'm the biggest disappointment of all times. "There's something going on, Kurt. Daniel *and* Billy think that you, or someone that looks a lot like you, is doing some sick shit. The police are looking for the guy. People are, like, *scared* and shit. I know Billy is fucked up and I want to help, dude, but you have to be honest with me. Is there something I should know?"

"What? Like I'm a fucking subway pusher? How long have we been friends? Yes, I'm depressed and fucked up and lonely but I'm not psychotic. I'm not fucking *crazy*. Believe me, if I were, you'd be the first to notice." I try to smile but it just comes out looking fake. "I appreciate you coming over and telling me, but there's obviously some big mistaken identity or something."

Sherlock paces around the room. He grabs the woodpecker boy's matchbook of all things from my shelf and casually lights one of the matches, watching it burn for a second before blowing it out. I want to smack his hand for using one of those precious matches.

"Put those back, please."

Sherlock rolls his eyes and tosses the matchbook back on the shelf. "There's something else, dude."

He stands up. "Okay, Kurt. If you're not going to talk, fine. But remember, I never asked to be pulled into all this shit. I have a *career* to worry about. You guys push each other in front of trains for all I care, but leave me out of it, okay?"

"Okay. Enough about your career, dude. You tell me that all the time."

"That's because it's important."

I just stand there, not moving. Suddenly, there's a knock at the door. What's next? Don't tell me I'm going to be tag-team interrogated by Sherlock *and* Billy.

"Are you going to answer the door?" Sherlock asks.

"Yes," I utter and pull open the door to find Pete standing there with his glasses on, shirtless, his perfect chest and beaming smile spilling into my dysfunctional space. His hair is even wet, fresh and clean from the shower. He almost looks like a fucking male model, I realize for the first time. He's too perfect in that pretty-boy way. I don't even know what to think of him. Every time I try to imagine being his boyfriend, all I can picture is drinking coffee at eight a.m. and watching him do sit-ups on one of those blue inflatable exercise balls.

Sherlock stares at him in disbelief. He's always had a secret sex thing for this type, even though he'd never admit it. I give him a minor mean look for ogling Pete. For the first time, I feel some sort of possessive pull over him. If he falls for Sherlock, I'm really fucked.

"Hi," Sherlock says, smiling. Sherlock never smiles; this is bad. "You're such a contemporary

Clark Kent." He laughs. "I'd love to paint you."

Pete laughs nervously. "Hey Kurt, I was just stopping by to see if you wanted to, like, take a walk to the park or something?"

"I can't. I have to work," I respond without thinking. I regret saying it as soon as I'm finished. The idea of a walk to the park with Pete sounds kind of awesome.

"Well, stop by if you wanna take a break. I'm just going to rent some movies." He smiles at me.

Sherlock looks jealous, a total first.

"Is Jody back?" I ask, wondering if Pete and I would have the apartment to ourselves if I stopped over.

"She gets back tomorrow morning, so. . . ." He winks.

God, why he'd have to ruin such a cool moment? I guess this is never going to work with him, partly because he's just so fucking mainstream. "Come here please." I pull him into the hall. "What do you want from me, Pete? You're like this perfect guy. Look at you. Why would you want to waste your time liking someone like me? I'm a fuck-up. I can't provide anything you need. I mean, you're so, like, I don't know, *together*, and I'm . . . I don't know."

"Dude, but I *do* like you. That's all that matters. Don't count me out because I earn a living and I go to the gym and I take showers and shave. Come on."

"I don't know why, man, but . . . I don't know how to be the boyfriend of someone like you."

"Yes you do. Think about it." He smiles and walks back into Jody's apartment.

I walk back to my apartment to find Sherlock reading the first chapter of *Push*. "What is this, Kurt? I'm serious. Is this true?"

"Of course it's not true." I try to sound really honest. I mean I'm not lying, technically. I never pushed a skateboarder. I'm *not* Elliot Collinsworth no matter how much I identify with him sometimes.

"Dude. Listen to me. Daniel says he saw you almost push some kid. Billy saw you *seriously* push another dude. The *Post* says that at least one more dude has been pushed. And now I find your *novel*, and it's about a pusher. What do you expect me to *think*?"

I stand up to hug him and he avoids me by acting like he has to put his hat on that exact moment. "Nothing. It's all made up. It's art. You've painted pictures of dead boys. Did you murder them?"

"Dude, I'm just having a hard time explaining all this away. I gotta think about this shit. But I gotta go now," he says. "Zanig's having one of his famous artists' dinners tonight at the gallery. Everyone will be there." His voice is sort of zombie-like as if he can't really hear what he's saying. "Like, I don't know . . . everyone. . . . " He trails off.

"I thought you hated that kind of shit."

"You'd go if you were invited."

"You're right. Only I'd never be invited, so I don't have to worry about it. Call me after if you wanna come over and have a beer. I'll be here all night, as usual."

"Okay, man." He walks to the door, looks at me for a good two or three seconds without saying anything, and then opens the door. "If you're going to be in all night, why don't you go over and hang out with Pete? He seems nice. You could use someone like that." He closes the door behind him. Sherlock's calling people "nice?" What the fuck is happening to the world.

I plop down on my bed and my ears are ringing. It feels like they've been ringing since I pushed Robin. I like the sound of his name. I think of the bird and then I think of him strutting down the street. I get up and go to my computer to Google him. I type his name in and one entry comes up: a mention of him DJing at Mama's bar. There's no photo, so I just stare at his name, and then I think of him lying there on the cement. That poor dude. I hope he's okay. He's going to miss his gig tonight.

Billy is going to start telling people about what he saw me do. He's got the biggest mouth in the world. I have to convince him that Robin fell into the train, like he passed out or something, and somehow I just happened to be there, that I didn't push him and that Daniel the fucking yarn artist is out of his mind. I stop to examine it myself in the mirror. I don't *look* crazy.

I grab my keys and wallet, and replenish it with another $100 from the lady that got hit by the taxi, and head toward the L train, the closest subway station to my house. I didn't want to ride it for a while, but I can't really avoid it unless I repair my bike tire or somehow come up with a fuckload of cash to take taxis all the time. I slink down the subway stairs, looking around for cops. I flip the turnstile and sneak down to the Brooklyn-bound L train platform, which is full of people who live in Manhattan but have been convinced there's a better scene in Williamsburg. Good riddance.

I steer clear of everyone else on the platform so no one sees my face. I'm twenty-five feet away from the closest person, a loud girl and her friend dressed up for their night out.

The train glides in, quieter than the F or the A train, newer, with a white and blue interior and electronic signs. I step into the car and sit down across from an old Russian lady. Her face looks like a potato and she's knitting a pink scarf, presumably for her granddaughter . . . for this winter? Down the car are five multiple-bandana-adorned twink boys so skinny that I'm not positive they aren't really girls. They're all wearing white jeans and American Apparel tank tops. I lower my face so they can't get a good look at me, not that they've even looked my way.

I brace myself for the underwater tunnel, a tube under the East River. Every once in a while, an irrational fear of the tunnel tube buckling fills my entire body with dread. It comes on like the train itself approaches the station, fast and strong and direct without hesitation. The lights in the train suddenly blink off and on, something that never happens anymore, which is enough to inspire total panic. My hands are clammy and I feel like I might suffocate. I try to hide my panic from the Russian lady who is now obviously giggling at me, not that she could care less. Shit. I might really pass out. I can't think clearly. By the time the subway reaches Bedford Avenue, I'm feeling almost sick to my stomach.

Desperate to get out, I fling myself from my seat and race to the exit.

I climb the steps and walk straight to Billy's apartment, past an anorexic twenty-year-old boy on a razor scooter screaming, "Hark! Hark!" I roll my eyes. If there's a new "it" phrase, this skinny fashion victim — decked out in three ripped up layers of T-shirts with a Mountain Dew fanny-pack — would know it.

I walk up to Billy's building, a six-story brick tenement. I walked by here a couple of times after he group-emailed his new address, no doubt forgetting I was on the list.

I once wrote a poem about standing outside looking up at his windows, which were covered in these strange red and pink curtains, made by the textile artist no doubt.

My neck hurts trying to see you,
A person who makes me hurt more.
Those red curtains make me hurt, too,
But not as much because they're funny
And they tell me that you have pain, too.

I guess it's not the most refined poem on earth, but at the moment I wrote it, it really helped me move on. Or so I thought. Nothing was clear to me in that immediate post-Billy era. That was when that movie *Elephant* came out. Consequently, that blond kid who wears the yellow T-shirt with a bull on the front will always remind me of feeling like total rejected shit. I kept seeing a kid who looked exactly like him around the city for months afterward, always in the same yellow T-shirt with his baby chicken colored hair pushed behind one ear. I followed him around, on and off subways, in and out of Washington Square Park, down to SoHo, across Chinatown. It wasn't him — meaning the real guy — but still, I followed. There was a point where I didn't know what I would do during the day if I wasn't following someone. I didn't only follow the *Elephant* kid. I followed students. I followed money managers into Armani Exchange. I followed a woman dressed in a chef's outfit into Dean & Deluca and then down to Broome Street. I kept expecting someone to notice me, but they never did. I followed my friends, most of them ex-friends, people that I knew from art school and people I smoked with once in the stairwell as we waited for crits to begin. I even followed the textile artist and the guy who I learned was his new boyfriend.

No one ever went anywhere very interesting, which was really depressing in a *what's the point of life* sort of way. They went into shops. They would pick out ink pens and art supplies, plan meetings, drink. Sneak into the back of Starbucks to piss but not buy anything. They would watch other people, too. Once, the textile artist was following some dude while I followed him. We formed a caravan, walking in circles around the West Village until the textile artist's subject finally broke it by just going home.

I don't think Billy is home. The red curtains are closed. There's a light on behind them, but that means nothing because Billy has a thing about leaving the light on when he goes out. He thinks the light will scare criminals away even though he was burglarized once with the lights and the television on, on like a Wednesday night.

I'm soaking wet with sweat, my T-shirt is painted on now, my nipples showing through the fabric. I have to move on. I could easily stand here all night and feel really sad and cry and laugh and fall down into an enormous emo hole that would be hard to climb out of, but I can't indulge my emotions anymore. I walk back up to Bedford Avenue, trying to find some semblance of a bright spot in this horrible fucking day.

Sherlock is at his art dinner, and I certainly can't crash that without getting bitched out seriously. Plus, they'd never let me in the gallery. I'm not important enough to be taken seriously by those assholes.

I walk up toward the Metropolitan, a local homo bar, to look for Billy. Besides, I need a drink fast before I collapse in on myself. On my way there, I remember I could buy dope in this neighborhood. I know of a place just a couple blocks up and for once I have the fucking money. I walk around the triangle known as "dogshit triangle," a wedge-shaped park below the Brooklyn-Queens Expressway nicknamed this because of all the, you guessed it, lots of dogshit on the ground. No one's out, not even the ex-cons rumored to be let off here by the Riker's Island buses. No one. And it's pitch black, too. Even the subway entrance lights are out.

Slowly I realize that the power is out on the south side of the triangle. I go back down Metropolitan Avenue, just marveling at the dark and light. The south side of the street, on my left, is dark. The right side still has power. It's actually sort of beautiful looking. I could probably come up with some profound metaphor about this, but I'm too tired.

At the corner of Metropolitan and Bedford Avenues, I find myself standing in the front of an old indoor pool known as the Metropolitan Public Baths. It's basically an old natatorium, a square post office looking building with ornate columns and the name carved proudly overhead in the marble. The letter U in *public* is a V because it's supposed to be Greek or Roman I think.

I walk up the front steps and peer inside the glass door. It's dark except for the red emergency exit lights. As I lean on the door looking, it falls opens with a click.

I step into the lobby. The scent of the chlorine makes me feel calm, I guess because I used to be a swimmer in high school.

Except for my few friends, my swim team brothers were the only ones who didn't think I was weird. Without them, I would have felt way more lonely throughout middle school.

They didn't care to judge each other because in the lanes of the pool, we were all the same. You couldn't even tell us apart. That was comforting to me, to be anonymous. And the swim team was super low-profile, like most girls didn't even know the team existed so I never had to pretend to be interested in some chick because there was never a girl around period, unlike, say, the football or basketball team.

One of my swim brothers, the best swimmer on the team, a super pale, blond Russian immigrant kid named Boris, was a homo, even though he would have never admitted it.

Me and Boris would smoke pot after swim practice in his enormous bedroom (he said his dad got rich importing caviar to the U.S. market) and then we'd make out and jerk off together, sometimes to pictures of Eastern European boys in magazines.

Those stoned afternoons saved my life, even though I didn't love Boris and I never could have. He was just the only guy I had. I wouldn't have even been friends with him if he wasn't a homo. He pronounced my name like *cut*. I don't know how he made it through school with his accent, it was so strong.

Because we hardly ever talked, I was able to project my idea of the perfect person onto him. I imagined him liking my favorite books, my favorite bands and painters. I imagined him cooler than he ever could have been in reality.

Boris is probably married to a nice Estonian girl now. I'm sure he probably remembers me as some weirdo, if he remembers me at all.

Walking past the entrance desk — the sign-in sheet still lying open in a blue binder — I enter the big pool room. It's like a darkened cathedral — still and monumental — making the room almost impossible to see, just a thin sheen of grayish moonlight coming in the high, small windows.

I step to the edge of the pool, my arm midnight blue in the almost darkness, and dip my hand in the water. It's cool — amazingly refreshing. Instantly, I feel really loose and comfortable for the fist time in weeks, maybe months. All my problems — Robin and Billy and Sherlock and everything feels really far away. The only sound is a gentle slap of tiny waves hitting the sides of the swimming pool, caused by the gentle rumble of the subway passing in the ground below. That, and the sound of my breathing. I slide off my shoes and socks and then unbutton my pants and slide them off, too. I stand up just wearing my boxer shorts. They're Jaws II patterned, a great white depicted to look like it's coming out of the fly. I've had them 100 years. Any normal person would have thrown them out long ago. I can't for some reason. I slide down my boxer shorts and stand naked in the enormous room. It's a powerful feeling for some reason, and it feels more important somehow, like I've discovered a secret sanctuary, like it's an ancient temple, part of something bigger.

Then I sit down on the tile floor. I lie back and close my eyes, feeling the coolness of the titles on my back. The silence and stillness of the room are the perfect panacea for how shitty I've been feeling. My body totally relaxes for the first time in months.

Suddenly I hear something — a scuff on the floor, maybe just a filter switching on? I lift my head. It's too dark to really see anything, but as my eyes adjust, I see a figure standing in the doorway. Fuck. Is there no such thing as privacy in New York?

I reach for my T-shirt, but before I can pull it on, a scratchy male voice asks, "Who are you?"

"The door was open," I say, my voice quivering. "I just came in here trying to cool off."

The figure moves across the other side of the pool. He must have followed me in.

I can tell he's a dude, maybe in his twenties. I hear the rustling sound of clothes coming off — the metal clink of a belt buckle hitting the floor — followed by the soft sound of underwear falling down legs, then a gentle dive into the water.

The boy comes up, takes a deep breath, and almost grunts, or moans, like the water feels good.

I just sit here still, waiting to see what happens next. The concept that this could turn out to be somewhat interesting or sexy flashes in my brain. I feel guilty or . . . *something*.

"Get in. It feels amazing," the guy says.

I don't think. I just react. I jump in with my T-shirt balled up in my clenched hand. The water is almost too cool and I've never felt so refreshed. It's 1,000 times better than my bathtub.

The boy swims over near me, treading water. I can see now that he has short black hair, ghoulish-looking in a funny way, and he's got tattoos on his chest and upper arms.

I finally gather enough courage to swim right up to him. What I see first is a pierced lip — sort of sexy, sort of tragic, a bit trashy.

"What are you doing here?" he asks.

"I just tried the door and it was open." Impulsively, I move in on him and wrap my arms around his bony shoulders and look into his dark eyes. I never do anything like this, so I'm probably just as surprised as this kid must be.

He stares at me, like he's analyzing my face, thinking what to do next. He smiles and kisses me hard. It's like fucking perfect, his mouth grinding into mine and his tongue inside my mouth. He pulls me back a tiny bit then and pushes me underwater, fast and without hesitation. My face goes under and I accidentally suck in some water and feel like I might drown until he pulls me back up. I'm coughing and my throat stings. He's a fucking killer! The headline will read "Brooklyn Drowner Kills East Village Pusher." Finally, he lets me up. I gasp for air, coughing in fits. It hurts. "Fuck, I almost drowned," I shout, pushing my hair out of my face.

He doesn't respond. Instead, he just swims across the pool and treads water in the deep end, daring me to follow.

I follow him, fast, direct and without caring that he could be some psycho. I'm pissed but turned on at the same time.

He takes hold of my boner. He then slides down my pants and starts to jack me off. It's fucking majestic; it feels so good to have someone touching me.

I reach down and grab his dick and start to jerk him off a little. Our mouths meet and we begin grinding our lips together. I accidentally pull his lip piercing and I taste blood. Blood mixes with our spit. It's like I've found Ben after all these years. He even looks like what I imagine Ben would look like today.

We keep kissing, almost like we're keeping each other alive by CPR. I'm afraid if I stop, all this will disappear. I can't hold myself back any longer. I cum in his hand and he cums in mine. It's transcendent. I'll never be the same.

"What's your name?" I ask, blissed out for a second. God, this is easier than I ever realized.

He reaches up and hangs from the diving board by his arms, doing backwards pull-ups. "Scooby."

"Cool," I say, still a little out of breath.

Suddenly, a loud metal clang echoes through the hallow pool room.

"Who's in there?" a loud, super-masculine voice you only hear in New York calls out.

We try to be as still as we can under the diving board, but my heart is beating like crazy. Not only am I trespassing, I'm naked in a swimming pool with a boy I don't know during a blackout. This is not going to look good.

Sherlock saying *Billy said he saw you push someone* echoes through my brain like the bullshit indie hit of the summer. Last summer it was *Clap Your Hands Say Yeah* or some shit.

Keys jangling, flashlights probing the darkness, two cops walk into the pool room.

Holy fucking shit. I climb out of the pool and grab my boxer shorts and step into them as fast as I can. I slip with only one leg in and fall on my side, trying to catch myself with my hand. It hurts like hell. I think I sprained my wrist.

"Remain still!" one of the cops yells.

I sit down and let the pain cycle through and then I slide my other leg into my underwear.

The cops shines the flashlight on me just soon enough to catch a view of my dick. It's totally mortifying.

The other cop, a woman I think judging by her silhouette, stands to his side. "You're trespassing on New York City Parks and Recreation property."

Relief comes over me like a bucket of cool water. They're here because of *that*, not because I'm the pusher.

"Keep your hands where I can see them!" the male cop shouts.

The room's lights flip on, brighter than I ever would have thought they'd be, like an indoor basketball court.

The male cop orders us both to get dressed. Then he cuffs me and Scooby together like some wimpy chain gang.

Once we're sitting in the backseat, I look at Scooby for some sort of connection — a laugh, smile, whatever — but he just gives me a bothered look — like having sex in the pool was my idea. He turns his head toward the window away from me.

The female cop gets in the car and I plead, "Can't you just let us go with a warning?"

"We could, but what fun would that be?" she answers.

"Please?" I beg.

"Shut up," Scooby snaps. "They're not going to let us go. They're cops."

We're driven to a non-descript-looking police station nearby and go through the usual bullshit they put everyone through — fingerprints, mug shot, and the phone call. But who am I supposed to call?

Billy's is the only number I can remember unfortunately — because he's the one who's going to give me the hardest time about getting in trouble. Plus he thinks I'm a subway pusher, so I'm not thrilled with the idea of asking him to meet me at the police station. I dial his number slowly. I hear two rings, three, four. I know that voicemail is a very real possibility in about one second.

"What?" he answers, as if he was expecting my call and it's annoying to him.

"It's me. I'm totally sorry to call you like this but yours is the only number I could remember. I realize you hate me and wish I'd die, but I really, really need your help. I'm in trouble. I got caught trespassing in the Williamsburg Pool. The door was unlocked. I was hot. Now I need bail."

"Which jail are you in?"

"Greenpoint. It's near your house, I think."

"How much bail do you need?"

"I don't know. Bring your credit card just in case. I swear I'll pay you back. I'm really sorry. I had no one else to call."

"I don't know why this is my problem. I'll be there in fifteen minutes." He hangs up.

Tears form in my eyes. I'm so completely alone in the world that I have to turn to someone who hates me for help. Truly pathetic. They lead me to a windowless room to wait. They put Scooby in the next room over.

A really young-looking punk rock kid wearing filthy pants and a tanktop stares down at his feet. A fat man with no pants on is leaning into a corner, snoring. He stinks of hard liquor, which makes it almost impossible for me to breathe.

I can hear the cops talking, slightly muffled. They're talking about someone's birthday and how they're meeting at some Irish bar after their shift. Then a young-sounding male cop interrupts, "Whoa. There was another one. He was just found, twenty-two-years-old, NYU student. Broadway-Lafayette F stop. This dude's insane."

I'm startled by the metal holding cell door swinging open suddenly.

I'm crouched down on the floor, looking like the lamest criminal ever to set foot into jail.

A cop, tall and blond with a tattoo on his finger of a four-leaf clover, looks at me. "You got sprung."

"I get to leave?"

"Yeah buddy, up and out." He escorts me out and into an office, where I have to sign a form and get my wallet, keys.

"I overheard the other cops talking. Was someone else pushed?" I ask.

"Yup. Second this week. Right this way." He points to a door that leads into a glass-fronted low-rent lobby, where I see Billy pacing the lobby, wearing a corduroy hat that used to be mine, carrying that fucking stupid textile-artist bag.

He looks me up and down. "What the fuck, man?

What have you gotten yourself into now?"

"It was just trespassing. I told you. Can we just get out of here?"

He follows me out the door. "*We're* not going anywhere. You can take the bus. You're so lucky I didn't tell them what I know."

"It wasn't me!"

"Dude, I was watching you."

"A kid was pushed while I was arrested. I heard the police talking about the whole thing. Go in and ask them."

"I don't have time for this shit." He walks over to his new Volkswagen GTI, and before he gets inside, he says, "You owe me $1,000."

"Wait! Billy! Don't leave like this. Come on, don't you want to get a beer or something? I'm too hopped up on adrenaline to go home."

He gets in his car and rolls down the window. Right before he gets into the waiting GTI, not even looking back at me, he says, "You really need to find a replacement for me, dude. This is getting so old."

The headlights switch on and he drives away.

For the first time tonight, I look up at the sky. All the stars are out, twinkling above the Manhattan skyline. God, for such a shitty day, it sure does look beautiful.

Chapter Seven
The Heaviness of My Thoughts

The next afternoon, I get out of bed naked and look outside. The city is sparkling and clear. The light is so pristine that it almost hurts my eyes to look out the window.

Suddenly, my door flings open, hitting the wall behind it, knocking a book from the shelves above my bed. "You here?" Sherlock sticks his head inside, scaring the shit out of me.

I try to hide behind my desk chair, but it doesn't work.

Sherlock walks in, looking horrified. "Dude!" he screams. "You're naked."

"No shit. How'd you get up here?"

"I have a key, remember dumb ass? I saw your boy Pete in the hallway." He grabs one of the beers out of my refrigerator and opens it with the bottle side of a wine corkscrew. He takes a long drink and then makes that *ah* sound that people think they're supposed to make after they take a long refreshing drink.

"He's not my *boy*."

"It's obvious he's really into you."

"Yeah well, I'm not interested."

"Dude, he likes you. He's liked you for months. Give him a chance."

"He's lame," I say, tying my robe closed.

"He's cute. But whatever, listen: I needed to see you. We've got to talk hardcore, man. You're about to let your life go very badly and you're not doing anything about it."

"What?" I sit down at my desk chair, my thinking chair.

"Billy told me about last night. He said it was the last straw, you know? He's saying he's going to talk to the police if you don't. I don't know what to think. I know you're depressed, but you're not a murderer, or *attempted* murderer, or whatever. You need to get off your ass and deal with this."

"Deal with what?"

"With him. He's telling the cops he saw you push some dude into a train."

"That bullshit again? Didn't you hear about that other dude who got pushed? It happened last night while I was being held for trespassing. I totally got some action last night, by the way. Some hot mysterious dude."

"Good for you, but can we talk about that later?" he asks.

"Dude, all you need to know is that I didn't do it. I know I've done some crazy shit, but I'm not psycho."

"Oh really?" he asks sarcastically, like he's my prosecuting attorney, "Like when you tried to set a bomb off in Billy's apartment. Or when you tried to rape that Swedish photography student by slipping him a Roofie."

"Okay, I'm admitting I'm weird — I've made bad decisions — but I wouldn't *kill* someone."

"Then why do Daniel and Billy both think you would? They're convinced you're doing it. I don't get it. You have to tell me, man. Did you push that kid?"

"No. If you want to help me, talk to Billy. Tell him he's wrong. Please. You can convince him."

Sherlock stares out the window like he's thinking it over.

I stand next to him staring out the window and I notice these big puffy clouds. I hate the sky for being so beautiful right now. I flip it off. *Fuck you clouds! I hope you drop out of the sky. We don't want you here! I* glance at Sherlock, wondering why he's even here with me. I'm such a huge loser. "Where'd you see Billy anyway?"

"Smiths night. Didn't I already tell you that?"

"Did he show up with the *textile artist*?"

"The textile artist has a show coming up at Richard Luken Gallery. He calls them yarn paintings."

"What's with all the yarn lately? I'm totally yarned out. How do you take that crafty shit seriously?"

"It doesn't matter anyway. Billy hasn't been with him since last spring. He's with this chick, Wolfie. She's a musician. Just leave it alone."

"*She?* What do you mean?"

"Wolfie's a girl, dude."

"I can't fucking believe this shit. How long's it going to last with a girl? I never bought his fucking bisexual act seriously for a second. It's just style to advance his career. It's worse than bullshit, it's fucking dishonest bullshit." I pace around the room. And what, Billy's a fucking child molester now? If he's dating a nineteen-year-old at twenty-five, he'll be dating teenagers when he's in his thirties. Disgusting. I don't know what's grosser, the fact that she's a girl or that she's a fucking child. Images of Billy with some teenage boy attack me. The images flood my mind like a fucking iPhoto slide show — 69ing, mutual hand-jobs, back and forth sucking off. I have to stop this shit. I fucked a seventeen-year-old once. He seemed old though. That's what I told myself. He was a student at Stuyvesant, a real prick it turned out. He said he had herpes. Luckily I never got them. Stop, brain! Fucking stop for just one second. "I gotta get out of here, Sherlock. You wanna go get a beer with me? I like this bar just down the street. The bartender is cool."

"No thanks, man. I gotta work." He takes a deep breath. "You know, I figured you'd ignore what I came here to say. Billy's threatening to talk to the police and you're worried about him dating a girl? I already told you I don't have time for this. If you wanna talk, drop by my studio." He stands up and walks out without saying goodbye. He doesn't believe me. He's starting to hate me and he's the only person in this entire city I have left.

I don't blame him. I would have walked out, too. That's what sucks. I have only myself to blame.

I decide to do the decent thing for once and head down to the bar where Robin's friend works. I still don't know what happened to him and I want to know if he's okay or not.

The same dude is bartending. I don't know how to

casually bring up Robin, so I just blurt out awkwardly, "Holy shit, man. Did you hear? Your friend Robin
was in an accident. There's some major subway pusher out there. I heard he's got like three or four dudes
already. Shit. I'm, like, scared to ride the trains."

He walks up close to me and whispers, "Hold on
a minute. How do you know about Robin?"

"I read about it. It was in the *Post* or something."

"Are you serious? I didn't think any of the papers
reported it. I haven't seen anything. This is some
fucked up shit, a fucking *pusher*. It's like a '70s B
movie. I heard a kid died last night under an A train.
It's so weird." He brings me a beer.

"So is he okay, I mean Robin?"

"Yeah. He's got two serious black eyes and a
headache. His cheek's swollen. Luckily, his skull did-
n't crack, but there's a hairline fracture."

"Did he see the guy, the pusher or whatever?"

"No, but some kid walked by here the other day
and he saw Robin at the bar. He was all, 'I saw you
get pushed, dude.'"

"Shit, really? So did he tell him who it was or
whatever." *What the fuck?*

"He was pretty cryptic. He gave Robin his phone
number though. Said they should keep in touch. His

name was Billy." Shit. My expression turns morbid, I can feel it. I might pass out. I hope I don't look too freaked out. *Billy's talking to Robin.* I have to stop him. "Is there a phone in here?"

"Over there." He points to a payphone by the bathroom.

I walk over and dial and Billy picks up on the second ring.

"Hey. It's me," I whisper, turning away from the bartender. "I heard you talked to that Robin kid."

"How long do you expect me to cover for you? A kid was seriously hurt. Another *died*. I told you before. I'm going to the police if you don't turn yourself in."

"Okay, I'll tell you what happened. I tripped and fell, and as I was falling, I almost dragged that dude down and that made him fall into the train. It was a total fluke. I felt so bad about it, I had to run away. Please don't tell anyone though. I haven't told anyone yet, not even Sherlock. It was a total accident. I feel horrible. I even checked on the kid. He's not hurt bad at all."

"You need help, Kurt."

"Come on, Billy, you *know* me." Just as I say that, Robin walks in the door, waving hello to the bartender. Fuck, the universe really rocks sometimes.

Billy hangs up on me.

I peek around the corner to get a better look at Robin. He has two deep purple black eyes and his left cheek is bruised and swollen. Holy shit. He's real. I feel like I need to make it up to him for what I did. I watch him from the payphone.

"Hey Finny," Robin says to the bartender.

"How you feeling?" They talk like they've been friends a long time.

"My fucking face hurts and I don't have insurance, so I can't afford to pay for the painkillers. It sucks."

I walk back to my stool at the bar where my beer is sitting, trying to seem normal or casual or whatever.

Robin looks at me, does a double-take, like he remembers me.

Fuck. I turn my head away from him, hoping he won't put his memory together of me on the platform that day.

"Do you have an Advil back there, Finny?" Robin asks the bartender. "My head is fuckin' pounding."

I just found my opening. I have six Vicodins in my apartment I was saving for a special occasion that never came. I fantasized that I'd take them with someone I loved actually. I look at Robin. "Hey dude, I overheard you saying you needed painkillers...."

"Yeah?" he responds.

"I have some Extra Strength Vicodin at my place. It's just down the street if you want to come get them."

"Seriously? That would be so cool. You don't even know how bad I need them." He searches my face like he's trying to figure something out. "Hey, don't we know each other?"

"Maybe. I think I've seen you around," I lie.

"Yeah? How?"

"I can't remember, but somewhere." God, I feel so stupid now for pushing him when I just could have laid on my meager charms and bribed him with pills. "I live just up the street. You wanna come over and get them?" He's going to say yes and I can't believe it. I imagined a situation like this — asking some cool, cute boy over to my house a million times — but I never thought it would happen again. Who cares if I'm using bait to get him there?

"Yeah. Let's go."

I stand up and he actually follows me out.

"I'll be around later," he tells Finny and waves goodbye.

We walk down the street without talking. I'm just wishing that all the snobs I went to art school with would scurry by right now as I walk with this hot kid to my place. Then they'll all assume I've got this fascinating life going on filled with fascinating people even though they'll never see it. We don't pass anyone I know, though, except for the normal homeless guy residents of the block. I wave to the deli worker just to act like I'm some sort of neighborhood fixture, that I know someone, so he doesn't think I never leave my apartment, which is the truth. "Here it is," I say, sort of like *ta da*!

He follows me up the stairs. When we get to my door, I sort of panic. There could be some weird shit left out in the open. "Can you wait here for just a second?"

He laughs. Good sign. "Sure."

I barge into my apartment, closing the door but not latching it, and start shoving dirty clothes under my desk. Then I straighten up my sheets just in case we end up on the bed. God, lust makes me think of some totally lame shit. I'm sure, *"in case we end up in bed."* I sound like a total frat boy dork. I might as well invite Robin to the fucking Caliente Cab Company, that theme park of a Mexican restaurant in the Village. We could share a two-person cactus lime margarita in a glass the size of an ice bucket. I must be nervous because I always think of this stupid shit when I am. It's some sort of temporary insanity to keep my brain busy so I don't cancel the whole thing at the last minute, which I used to be known for doing. Fuck myself over before someone else does.

I check my refrigerator — still four more beers. I take my smelly kitchen sponge and wipe every surface in the apartment, leaving the whole place with a slight scent of moldy oranges. Better than the smell of dirty clothes, I guess. I hide photos of Billy in my desk drawer and I set my journals on top of them, sort of a symbolic act, like smothering his face with all the heaviness of my thoughts. He deserves it.

Shit, I think. It's taken longer than I thought. Robin's just standing out there in the hall for at least two solid minutes. I turn my old box fan on high and then run to the door and open it, attempting to stand so that my measly arm muscles are flexed, ha. "Hey, come in. Sorry. It was a mess, so I just wanted to. . . I don't know. . . clean up or whatever."

I turn on my laptop and try to find something cool to listen to. I end up just letting it play Nirvana, which shows I'm old school, but not trendy, my favorite combination. I hope he doesn't think this means I like metal or, god forbid, *classic rock*. I take a deep breath and turn around. I can't believe this dude is standing in the middle of my apartment.

He looks more fragile and beat up than he looked in the bar.

"You want a beer?"

"Yeah, sure." He watches me get the beer out and try to find the bottle opener. It takes me a few minutes until I find it lying underneath the claw-foot bathtub of all places. It must have rolled over there somehow. I hand Robin his beer and he takes a swig. I want him to be nervous, too, but he's so obviously not. Maybe he hangs out with total strangers all the time. He's so cute that he probably meets boys like me three times a week and the only thing that interrupted his daily prowl was me pushing him in front of a subway train. I hope that's not true.

"So, what happened to you? You're pretty beat up."

"I got pushed into a subway train. I was in Brooklyn that day to meet this guy I met online, and I was just waiting, spacing out, and this dude shoved me really hard into the train as it was coming

into the station. I almost blacked out." He giggles
nervously.

"That sucks. I'm sorry."

"You don't have to be sorry. You weren't there."

"Yeah. . . . " I feel so shitty about lying to him. I *so*
want to tell him the truth, but I know he'd bolt and
tell the cops on me.

"I'm sorta sick of talking about it if you don't
mind. Hey, are those Vicodins around? I could really
use a couple." He sits down on my bed.

"Oh yeah, sorry." I open my top desk drawer and
find them sitting in a little wooden box from
Chinatown. "Here you go," I say as I hand him all six
of them.

He takes two right away, washing them down with
beer. "Thanks."

"No problem, man," I steal glances at him. He's so
fucking cute I can't stand it. He's looking at me sort
of flirty, too, sort of too direct.

"Dude, do you want to like...make out?"

Shit. I'm bright fucking red and burning hot, and
my courage soars for thirty seconds. "What?"

"You know, like. . . . "

"Yeah man. Come over here." He motions me over
to my bed, where he's sitting. I really can't believe

this is happening. I feel like a camera crew is going to pop out from the closet at anytime.

Okay. Stop it.

Once I'm on the bed, he slides right up to me.

He turns toward me and kisses me. "I think you're really hot." He rubs my thigh and slides his hand between my legs as we kiss. "And you smell hot, too."

It's too fast. Up close with all the scabs and the black eyes, he looks like a monster. It's weird.

My door buzzer rings, triggering my adrenaline double-time.

"You're not going to answer that, are you?" he asks.

"No." Answering the door is the last thing on my mind right now. I've never been kissed so perfectly. I reach over and slide my hands under his shirt and up his smooth torso. He smells like stale beer and cigarettes.

"Kurt?" a male voice calls from outside my door. I think it's Billy. Fuck!

"Be quiet, okay?" I whisper to Robin. He nods.

"Kurt, I know you're in there! Open up!" This is the first time that I've ever wanted Billy to go away. "I saw Pete in the hall. He said you're home. Come on. . . ."

I lie as still as possible, not saying anything.

Robin doesn't move either. He's just listening and breathing softly.

"I heard you went and met Robin. You're such a weirdo. What are you trying to achieve?"

I turn my head away from Robin and close my eyes. This is the worst possible timing in my entire life. Billy better not say what I think he's about to say.

"I saw you push him, Kurt."

Holy fucking shit. It's happening.

"Why'd you do it? I don't understand you anymore. Why are you ignoring me?!" He bangs on the door and I can tell he's pissed off. "Fine. Fuck it. I'll just scream it through the door. Go into the precinct by your house and tell them what you did. You have to face this like a man for once. They'll go easy on you because you're being honest. If you don't tell them, I will. I'll give you forty-eight hours to do it. I'm serious, Kurt. I'm not fucking around."

I hear Billy take off down the stairs. I take a deep breath and wish I could just disappear. How am I going to get out of this in front of Robin?

"What was that about?" He looks at me accusingly. "You're the dude who pushed me?" He looks almost scared.

"No, dude, of course not. That was my ex-boyfriend. He's totally crazy and he's out to get me."

"But why would he think that? That was Billy, right? He's the guy who saw me get pushed. He rode in the ambulance with me and waited for me in the ER waiting room until I was released and then he drove me home. He was like my guardian angel."

"I'm sorry that happened to you, dude." I lean in and try to kiss him on the mouth, but he pulls away. "You don't deserve it."

Robin stands up. "What the fuck, dude? What's going on here?" He looks like he's going to burst, he's so confused. "I gotta take off," he says, already moving toward the door, a thin coat of sweat on his forehead, a haunted look on his face. He leaves right away, closing the door behind him.

Once he's gone, I panic, pacing around my tiny apartment. My world is closing in on me, surrounding me like those rangers circling that coyote in Central Park. It died of course. I should just jump in front of a train and end it, make life a lot easier for everyone I know.

Chapter Eight

The Life
I Could
Be Living

It's getting dark. It's been three hours since Robin left.

I stand up and look outside. There's a cop car parked across the street. They're probably watching me, ready to pounce. I'm sure they've got my phone tapped already. I dial Billy's number again and leave a message — my fifth. I've got to talk him out of telling the cops. "Billy, why do you want to ruin my life? You're the one person I thought I could count on. Please don't do this to me. Can we talk about it? Please call me back. I love you." I hang up. This sucks. The only person I thought I would live the rest of my life with is threatening to ruin my life. I pick up the phone to try him again. His message comes on right away, which means he pushed *ignore* on me.

I can't hang around here waiting for the police to show up. I need to see Billy right away. If I can actually find him — and I think it's not too late — I think I might be able to talk him out of this shit somehow.

I decide to stay away from the subway, so with $200 and credit cards left from the wallet I stole, I'll take a cab. I'll try one of the lady's credit cards. If it's been cancelled, I always have cash and it shouldn't cost more than $20 to get over to Williamsburg.

I open my desk drawer to find the credit card from the woman's wallet. As I grab the beautiful sparkly plastic credit card, I catch a glimpse of the lady's driver's license. She actually looks really cool — warm, old but still pretty. I hope she didn't die, poor woman. Cabbies drive like assholes.

I pull on a clean T-shirt and take off outside.

A cab sits right outside my apartment building, so I jump in the back and direct the driver to Williamsburg. The trip only takes ten minutes, and when I hand the cabbie the stolen platinum card, he sighs because they all hate credit cards apparently. He grudgingly swipes the card on his cellular credit card reader, equipped with a little rubber antenna.

I wait for the card to be rejected, but instead, the receipts start cranking out of the little machine.

Maybe the lady *did* die. She would have cancelled the card if she were alive. Fuck.

"Thanks," I say, as the cabbie hands me the card and the slip to sign on a little clipboard. As I step outside into the hot night, I half expect some undercover cop to run at me from an unmarked American sedan, but no one does. The neighborhood is strangely quiet — no electro-clash music, no Razor scooter relay races, no ironic red rover games on the street.

I think about the life I could be living here with Billy. We'd be drinking a beer about now, maybe a little hungover from going out the night before. We'd be talking about what to eat for dinner and someone like Sherlock would stop by later with a six-pack. We'd watch something on television, then go to bed feeling safe in our peaceful apartment.

I'm more than a little embarrassed by these stupid bourgeois dreams. I hate craving a boyfriend and security, when to almost everyone I know, I pretend that I despise everything about a settled life.

But I can't help it. Billy and I used to be so happy together. We were one of those couples that everyone said was cute, that made people — even loser fags — optimistic about love. But after his band became big, that didn't last long. He tried to convince me that sleeping around was part of being in a band — part of his artistic process — and that if I didn't like it, I should find a boyfriend with a boring job. Eventually, I stopped obsessing over clues that he was fucking someone else because I didn't want to know. Until his music took off, we talked about moving to Portland, Oregon, where he was from. I thought this would settle him down, I guess. He was always a little weird, he claimed a little disconnected from reality. His parents had died in a car accident on the way to his high school graduation, leaving him basically with no one and a small life insurance policy. He said he wanted me as his family and I believed him. Considering my shitty parents, I needed him as my family, too. He was totally amazing at sex, practically an athlete, always concerned about how I felt more than himself.

I guess things began to fall apart between us before his band became big. I overlooked parts of him I didn't like because I liked him so much. He always needed new people around, so I never found him to be that loyal to his friends. He'd ditch people for new friends all the time.

After we broke up, there was a month of silence between us. I tried — I really did — to move on with my life. I promised myself I would not call him, not after cheating on me like that, and I actually stuck to it for a while. I began to forget about him. I started to feel better. Then he phoned me every night for a week straight crying, telling me how much he missed me, how much he missed my jokes and my weird personality and of course, the sex. I fell in love with him all over again that week. I pleaded with him to move back in with me, but he said he couldn't handle it. He said it would be too hard for him to take.

Out of nowhere, Pete comes into my mind — his dark brown eyes and perfect slender torso. He's the anti-Billy, which may account for my unexplained attraction to him. It's like Pete sees some golden quality deep inside me someplace, so deep that I can't even see it. I wish I could hug him right now. I think I could trust him.

Before that thought digests, I've arrived at Billy's building. Looking at it, I remember when this city offered so much promise, so much hope, to me at least. Now its old buildings, crowded streets, and rumbling subways feel like they're cementing me in, trapping me in a state of pure depression. It makes being broke and sad feel bigger, even monumental. Everything is bigger in New York.

I wipe my eyes with the bandana from my back pocket. I can't look like this when I see Billy. He's seen me cry too many times already. It doesn't even faze him anymore.

Billy's lights are on. I've walked past here seventeen times without ever once ringing the buzzer. This time I'm just going to hit the fucking button. I have no choice. I walk right up to the door, find his name, and press the buzzer.

A female voice answers. Wolfie, that slut child-bride. She should be dating a stockbroker, someone with a future, anyone but the train wreck that is Billy — and me calling someone a train wreck, that says a lot.

"Hey. Is Billy there?"

"Who's this?" the voice asks, playfully.

"His ex-boyfriend."

"Oh," she sounds surprised, "hold on." The speaker goes staticky for a minute. "Okay. I'm buzzing you in. We're on the third floor, front apartment." If that fucker never told this chick he was a homo for like fucking six years before her, I'm going to be seriously pissed off. As I start up to the third floor, I see a door swing open at the end of the hall and there stands Wolfie. She really is a girl. Wow. I didn't really believe it until now.

She looks about seventeen and she's actually sort of pretty. She holds her hand out and I lean in and kiss her instead. Power, I think. She's rail thin with black dyed short-cropped hair, not very feminine, a tom-boy or whatever. She's not wearing shoes, which I interpret as *she lives here*. She's also holding a camera, a Hasselblad 4x5, which means *art student*. Ugh. I've had way too many art students in my life already.

I can't believe fucking Billy let this chick move in with him.

"I was just shooting a nude of Billy, so he's gettin' dressed," she says, hitting all my buttons all at once. "So he'll be just a minute."

I look around, noticing three poster-size photos on the wall from a night that Billy and I spent walking around the city during the transit strike. They're images of closed down buildings, boarded up, chained and graffiti-covered. It was so cold that night. Seeing the photos feels like a punch in the stomach. They make me feel jealous and sad and angry and nostalgic all at once.

There's a lot of new shit around, too, a big sectional couch and a flat-screen TV, so I assume either Billy's band really is a big success or Wolfie's a spoiled rich kid. Or worse, both!

"So, you're his ex-boyfriend?" she asks, smiling. "You were the one in, like, *jail* the other night." *She knows nothing about me.* The most important person in my life has never mentioned me to his new girl-friend. I can't believe I'm even thinking the word *girl-friend*. It's like the life I had with him is wiped out, made frivolous, turned into some edgy back-story for him to talk about at parties to prove what a Bohemian he once was. He'll say *"I used to have a boyfriend"* and everyone will laugh, but later make fun of him behind his back because they think he's still a homo.

This was a mistake. I have to get out of here. "Where's the bathroom?" I ask, sounding a bit too close to panicking, although I'm sure she doesn't notice. She's a fucking *child*.

She points down the hall and I go, closing the door behind me.

I freeze in front of the mirror. I can't face Billy with his girlfriend here. It's like he just let me in to show off Wolfie, to make me feel stupid and inconsequential, to humiliate me before he turns me into the cops.

Focus, dumbshit! If he tells the police, you're screwed. Desperate, I open the medicine cabinet and there it is — a temporary solution at least — a bottle of Vicodin, prescribed to Wolfie Pamela Sutton by Dr. Robert Eisenman in Greenwich, Connecticut. *Take one to two every four to six hours as needed for pain.*

So Wolfie's a rich suburban girl? She probably pays the rent. *Her parents actually named her Wolfie?* I might explode. I take four Vicodins, wipe my eyes, and open the door, walking back into the room with what I hope looks like confidence.

Billy walks out from the hallway pulling on a black tank top.

I lose it. "What? You were taking naked photos with your *girlfriend*? What does that make me? Just some stupid mistake?"

He says very evenly — too calmly — like a therapist, "I told you from the beginning I was bi."

"I don't believe that for a second! That's what people say who don't want to admit who they want to fuck. It's so high school."

Billy doesn't even react. That's a bad sign. "Kurt. I can't worry about you anymore. I can't have you calling me three times an hour. I can't feel guilty about you getting mad at me and not forgiving me for hurting you. I don't think I can have you as part of my life anymore. You're on your own. You have to handle this shit on your own. Otherwise, you'll never figure it out."

Shit. I just lost my last best hope of talking him out of reporting me to the cops. I can't control myself around him — it's horrible. I wish I could take back what I said. "I'm *sorry* I ever needed you in the first place. I regret ever knowing you. You've hurt me more than you'll ever realize."

"I realize it, Kurt. I think you should go now."

"I'll leave when I'm ready to."

Wolfie stares at me like I might explode.

"Fine. Come with me." Billy leads me down the hall to his bedroom..

The first thing I notice is the dresser that used to belong to us. A photo of Billy and Wolfie kissing sits on top of it, framed, sitting on a dresser that used to be mine and his, which makes this emo-bomb I'm experiencing right now even more treacherous. The small top drawers used to hold our underwear and socks, all mixed together. We wore whatever we happened to pull out of the drawer. I open the drawer to find a line of panties folded neatly inside.

It's too much for me to take. The jealousy, the feeling of being fucked over and thought of as some stupid *phase*, rushes back like Katrina. I collapse onto the floor, sobbing, covering my face with my hands. How do I manage to fuck up every aspect of my life?

Billy stares at me for a minute. "I don't know what to do with you. I can't keep rescuing you. This has to be finished. I love you, Kurt, but please just let me go. Please? I think it's really fucking you up."

"Don't say that. I can't take it. It's too *conceptual*."

"I always worried you'd hurt yourself and that's bad enough, but hurting someone else? Going as far as you've gone? I won't let you."

I don't know how to respond. I just kneel on the floor burying my face in my arms.

"Do you think this is easy for me, Kurt? I don't want to lose you. I always imagined we'd be friends when the drama blew over. I imagined us knowing each other when we're old men. It kills me to turn you in. But you've given me no choice. I'm trying to help you get your life back."

"This is you helping? Then just stay out of my life."

"This can't go on. You *hurt someone*. Two dudes have died!"

"The guy who did that was fucking arrested. What happened with Robin was an accident. Just don't tell the cops and I'll leave you alone for good."

"I can't do that. We both know it was a lot more than an accident. Tell them by tomorrow or I'm going to."

I'm fucked and there's no way out of this. "Fine." I get up fast, wipe my eyes, and storm out into the living room. "I knew you didn't care! And you know what? You're a total fag! I don't believe you really want to fuck that girl for a fucking second!"

Wolfie is taking a photo of the television screen, of a shirtless muscular frat boy on some MTV *Road Rules* competition show. I'm having the biggest all-time meltdown of my life and she's making "art."

"Bye," she says like she's won.

"Whatever." I run downstairs, push the door open hard, and walk as fast as I can up to Bedford Avenue. I have to avoid a couple packs of trying-too-hard-to-be-cool teenagers taking up the whole fucking side-walk.

I head straight for the subway. I want to get out of this neighborhood as fast as possible. There's no safe-ty for me here, nothing calming. I jump three steps at a time down into the foul-smelling subway station. I scan the platform for anyone cool like I always do, except I can barely see because my eyes are stinging from saltwater tears. There are some girls who proba-bly just transferred from the G train, which always takes forever. They all look at me when I walk toward them, paranoid I think, about the "subway pusher" that the *Post* has started reporting on, romanticizing, even . . . like, *egging on.* I walk past them, faking a push with my hand on one of the girl's bare shoulder and laughing. The girls laugh back.

At the far end of the platform, I find a blurry kid, probably twenty, with that hair-in-his-eyes cut and that skinny pasty look with scratched up black painted fingernails, chewed short. He's all alone, looking intently down the tunnel, waiting for the train.

I slowly walk up behind him, just far enough away so that he won't move.

He's reading a paperback, so he barely notices me. He's the type who'd rather talk about Star Wars than anything else really.

I stand behind him, waiting for the train. I really want him to look at me, to like me in some way, to somehow at least notice me, acknowledge that I exist. Standing behind him, I lift my shirt up to my nipples, but he doesn't sense to turn around. I say, "Hey" like a karate jab, and sort of loud, and he doesn't even flinch. He keeps on reading his paperback, the doofus.

The headlights reflect on the polished tracks as the L train approaches the station, the screech of a track curve down the tunnel.

He takes a couple steps forward, closing his paperback and watching the train approach.

I reach my hand out, just inches from his back.

As the rumble gets louder and the train gets closer, I close my eyes and imagine pushing him, his back arching, falling headfirst off the platform.

I imagine him looking up at me before the train slices him in half, his expression confused, or like...he's seeing a ghost or something. I turn away and run up the stairs back out onto Bedford Avenue. My heart is going to explode. I'm drenched in sweat. I run south toward the industrial-age Eiffel Tower-looking Williamsburg Bridge until I spot an unchained delivery bike. I grab it and take off.

An Asian guy runs after me, screaming, "Hey, that's my bike!"

I pump the pedals as hard as I can, and then harder still. I ride up onto the bridge bike lane and fly back to Manhattan. I zip down Delancey Street and up Avenue B and leave the bike on the sidewalk.

I'm not out of breath when I reach the top like I normally am; instead, I feel a little high. I feel vital for the first time in forever, like I'm actually real. I know it's all involving bad shit, but it's sort of nice that people are at least thinking about me.

A minute later, someone knocks on my door. I have this feeling that bad news is on the other side of the door, but I manage to stand up and open it anyway. I let the door fall open and it's just Pete.

"Hey buddy. I heard you come in. . . . "

Before he can even finish, I throw my arms around him, letting the weight of my entire body fall into his. I nuzzle his shoulder and then start kissing him on the mouth. He begins kissing me back, then gets a little tentative, like he's sensing something's off about me. He pulls slightly away and looks me over. "Everything okay?" he asks.

I close my eyes. "Let's not talk about it, okay? Just don't leave. Please?"

He nods, a little concerned, and steps into my apartment.

Chapter Nine

The Sky Is a Deep Slate Gray

I wake up, a creeping sense of dread running through my body, with this sensation in my chest, the same feeling as when I was in high school, when I wanted to move here so bad. Even watching *Saturday Night Live* made me feel better because I got to see video of New York in the beginning where they introduce all the cast members. New York is the place I was meant to be and I made a life here, no matter how simple and boring it is. I struggled to get here. I worked all night long on my paintings, so I could get into Cooper Union. I used to have passion, I realize. I used to be the person I want to be now. When did I lose it? I guess every miserable person could look back and find the moment in time when they lost their way. I have to find mine. It's some-where on these streets, in this city.

I can't waste any more time. I'm living the dream I had since I was fifteen-years-old. That younger me would die if he knew I wasn't taking advantage of every second of my life.

I get dressed and go out to walk around, to just experience the city. It's raining again and the sky is a deep slate gray, which I like because I can cry if I feel like it without trying to hide it. My tears mix with the rain and I like the idea that they evaporate to the same place — where, I don't know. The air I guess. I grab a slice of pizza, because I realize I haven't eaten in almost two days.

I devour the slice in seconds, so I order another one and eat it just as fast.

I walk outside and walk right past a cop on his bike. He looks at me no differently than he'd look at any old person, no recognition whatsoever. Maybe I'm a fool to believe the police would actually think I'm the pusher. I spot the *Post* in a magazine stand, the headline reads *Suicide Note Found; Boy Not Pushed*. I buy it and open it to the article immediately.

This kid who everyone thought was pushed actually killed himself. I read his suicide note, sections of which are printed in his actual handwriting. He makes me sound normal.

I wish I could pull 1,000 other dudes in front of the subway with me and we could all die together in one hot violent bloodbath. Goodbye New York City. I fucking hate you and everything you stand for. Mom, Dad, Bro: You did nothing to help me and I sure as fuck don't have any friends, so this is it. Romantic, huh?

Wow, sort of post-modern — *romantic*? I wonder who knows him; the article says he went to Cooper Union two years behind me. I bet Sherlock knows him.

Shit. This is sort of like *getting to me*, this kid's note. I've like, been in his shoes, but not so far gone. What separates a kid like that from me? At what point did he transform from a whiny emo loser to this powerful, brave person who gave it all up to make a point? A stupid point, but still. I wonder if he snapped or if it was a gradual progression, little things wearing him down the way New York can wear anyone down. I wish I'd known this kid. I think I could have saved him. He sounds deranged to say the least, but us together, we might have been a little less fucked up. Even without knowing him, I know what he's been through. I'm sure he'd have felt the same way about me.

Now I feel like I need to get back to my apartment as soon as possible. I tried to go out and have a real day sort of like some normal person, but I'm just incapable of it I guess. Total failure. When I get back home,

I take a deep breath and plop down in my chair. It's getting dark outside, so I switch on a lamp and read some of *American Daze*, picturing Calhoun in motion, wondering if he'd really like me, fantasizing about how I'd like to visit him in his loft in an old — shit, I can't remember — is it a doll factory or a shoe factory? I think about how I wish I could take a shot with him, enter that heroin haze where everything that matters is within five feet of your reach. It's amazing I never became a raging heroin addict. It's probably the only thing I was ever strong enough to resist.

I did a little dope back during my freshman year of Cooper Union and got slightly hooked, did some Subutex for awhile and eventually got off it. During that period, something changed in my body chemistry. I never felt happiness the same way again. What once felt like happiness now isn't enough. It was as if I'd turned a corner and never found my way back. That's the thing with heroin — you have to keep doing it.

Calhoun shoots up and settles back in his chair to tell me how he's feeling — good and numb. Then he stands up and gets in bed with me, keeping me dazed in his warm cocoon for a pretty long time.

Chapter Ten

Never
See This
Room Again

The telephone ringing jolts me awake. "Hello?"

Pete, who's in bed with me, rolls over and covers his face with a pillow.

"You didn't do it, did you? You need to go to the police." It's Billy and he sounds done with me. But he *is* calling. That's a first for the month.

"Dude, I would never turn you in. You could murder Sherlock and I wouldn't say a word." I hope this sounds convincing. I actually believe it.

"If I murdered Sherlock, you *should* turn me in." He takes a deep breath, like he's annoyed with me. I'm so tired of annoying him. It totally zaps what little of my self-esteem still remains. "I'm coming over. I'll walk you over. I looked it up online. The ninth precinct is just a couple blocks down from you."

"Yeah, I've walked past it," I say, feeling totally defeated. What will they arrest me for? Attempted murder. Assault? What does pushing some prettyboy into a subway count as?

"I'm already close to your house, so I'll be there in fifteen minutes."

"Can you give me a half hour?"

"Yes, but that's it. You're going to be fine, dude. It's not like you killed someone. Did you?"

"No! Of course not. God."

Pete stirs in bed and then gets up and stumbles across the room to piss, his boxer shorts all crooked. I wave at him, rolling my eyes about my telephone conversation. He smiles and starts to piss.

"See you in thirty. And answer the door this time, Kurt."

"Okay, bye." I hang up the phone, feeling a strange sense of accomplishment for some reason. Then I start to panic inside. The police are going to arrest me. They're going to put me in a cell. Fuck.

Pete finishes peeing. "Who was that?"

"Billy. He wants me to go to this exhibit with him — his friend's show," I lie, and search around for a T-shirt to put on. I step into my jeans and fasten my belt.

"This early?" Pete slumps down on my chair, stretching and yawning at the same time.

"Yeah, he wants to go over there while they're installing it," I say. Why am I such a good liar?

"What are you doing later?" Pete asks, standing up and twisting his torso around like he's stretching for a marathon or something. "Do you want to have dinner or something?"

"Uh...yeah. Sounds good." And it does. I stick my wallet and keys into my pocket, trying to act like I'm leaving so Pete will give me a moment here alone. After all, I might not be coming back for a long time.

Luckily, he takes the hint. He pulls on his shirt and pants and kisses me. "See you later. I'm going back to bed next door." He smiles at me and walks out into the hall.

Once he's gone, I collapse on my chair and just sit here, totally still, taking it in — the apartment, the view of the building across the street where the heavy metal guitarist guy lives, the unwashed cups in the kitchen sink, the *Post* lying on the rim of the bathtub, my dirty boxers peeking out from under the bed, my three pairs of shoes beside them, my books.

Immediately, I grab Calhoun in his forever junk-aided *American Daze* from my nightstand and shove him in my backpack. I take a couple other books, stupid shit really, a book called *Love & Death*, a conspiracy about Kurt Cobain being murdered.

How do you pick your most cherished possessions in three minutes flat? I shove my laptop in with Calhoun.

I stand in the middle of my apartment, ready to never see this room again, and I think, I can't leave. I love this shitty apartment. I love my life, even though I complain about it every chance I get. It's like all of a sudden, I see my life in a new way, from a new angle. It's not really so horrible. It's even fun sometimes. It's romantic and punk rock and exciting and real, or it can be anyway. Sure, I'm a hermit with only two friends, but at least I have two friends and both of them are cool. At least I made it to New York, to have the joy of summers and winters living the life of an artist, a life ten times more interesting than the world of anyone I grew up with. I hold my keys, wondering if I should even bother taking them. Will I ever be back? I put them in my pocket.

I strap on my backpack, open the door, take a deep breath, and step outside my apartment, closing the door behind me. Wait. I can't leave without telling Pete where I'm going. I duck back inside my apartment and write a note. *Dear Pete, I think I might love you. I'll call you soon. I had to go away, for a while any-way. xoxooxoxox Always, Kurt.*

I slide the note under the door and hurry down the stairs for the last time for a long time. Every creak seems symbolic, important.

I count the steps for the first time in two years. Once I'm outside, it's me in the world, unprotected by the walls of my apartment, by those forty-eight wooden stairs. A meteor could fall on me, crushing me, and every thought I've ever had would disintegrate into dust.

I walk slowly, not the normal New York cruise-missile pace where you're too busy to look at anyone or anything. I take time to notice my surroundings, actually looking at all the interesting faces of people who walk past me. So many cool, ambitious people who moved here for the same reason I did, so many dreams realized every day, even more broken per-haps. The angle of the sunlight is starting to change as late summer comes into its own. Where once the sidewalk on Avenue A was always hot and sunny this time of day, it's now in the shadow of the four-story buildings alongside it.

I walk over to see the Astor Place cube sculpture to take my last look. I come up around the corner and

I don't see the sculpture. At first, I think a bus is just blocking it, but as the bus pulls away, the cement island where the sculpture normally sits is empty. Where the fuck is it? Where did it go? I run through deadlocked traffic to the island.

A couple of kids are looking at the rust-stained spot on the cement where the cube's base once stood.

I walk up behind them. "What happened?" I ask, to neither of them in particular.

The taller one turns around and says, "They took it away in the middle of the night."

Fuck. The cube is gone. It always seemed so permanent. I never fathomed it would ever be gone.

Chapter Eleven

I Should
Be Glowing

I pass through the rusting iron gates of Tompkins Square Park past some homeless punks smoking cigarette stubs, past a little boy with a cape swooshing down the asphalt pathway like he's flying.

I look up at the trees, majestic ancient statues patiently passing time, and I try to imagine what they've seen — men in top hats on horse-drawn carriages, the rise and fall of the stock market many times over, the ash and dust and screaming hoards of September 11th, when those giant buildings, ten times taller than the highest trees, collapsed in on themselves like enormous, malfunctioning robots.

I remember what I was doing that morning — I heard the first airplane clearly, lying in bed, thinking about what to eat because I'd woken up especially hungry. Billy and I were living together in Brooklyn.

He started crying when he found out and I'd never seen him cry before. He got a bottle of codeine from his backpack and we sat around all day and all night and watched the news like it wasn't happening just twenty-five blocks away. That night, he kissed me like he loved me. We had sex in front of the television while the death toll rose. Our orgasms were numbed by the codeine, but it still felt good.

I sit down on a bench for a few minutes, just to feel the warm air. As I cross my legs, this guy I always see around, this redhead dude who always wears a beret, walks past, on his way somewhere. We've never even acknowledged each other, but we see each other three times a week on the street outside my apartment. I wonder now why I never bothered to say hello. He looks like a nice enough guy. He's even cute.

I stand up. I need to get out of the neighborhood before Billy finds me.

I think about going to JFK, but where could I go? I only have $150 left. I don't think that's enough for even the shortest flight.

Fuck it. I can't leave this city that I wanted to live in all my life. This thing I have here, it's valuable. There are tens of thousands of kids all over this country and all over the world who would take my apartment away from me with thirty seconds notice, assume my lame life, wear my dirty clothes, spend what little money I have, take my friends, even my stupid sadness, and live happily ever after.

I walk slowly, peacefully I guess, down Avenue A. The city is waking up. No one pays any attention to me as usual and, I'm like, in this epic zone of emotions and feelings, and they don't even notice. I feel like I should be glowing, but I'm just another boy on the sidewalk. I *am* just another boy on the sidewalk and all my bullshit drama is nothing special. I'm nothing special. This makes me feel sort of good in a weird way. I fit in here. I'm a fucking weirdo and I'm normal here. That's what New York does for you.

I'm drawn to the subway, sort of to take one last look. I walk down the stairs, my backpack getting heavy. I swipe my Metrocard at the turnstile.

It's getting hot inside, already busy. People are going places. They're walking and waiting and listening to music, which makes this city an enormous epic movie, a million different varieties from wistful to ecstatic to trippy to forlorn to scary.

I walk down the center of the island platform, uptown trains on the right, downtown trains to Brooklyn on the left. A five-foot drop off runs down either side where the gleaming tracks run next to the third rail, which a sign warns is high-voltage, instant death if touched. It's so *easy* to fall in there, I'm amazed it doesn't happen more often.

An uptown train arrives, the shrill electronic beep of the doors opening, commuters pouring out only to be replaced by a new army of riders. The doors close. The people are taken away. No one even looks at me. I want to shout to everyone, "Look, it's me! The pusher!"

I'm so overwhelmed that I can barely stand. I feel like I'm almost gone. I'm almost just like blending in to the city, like trashcans on the corner, gum spots on the sidewalk, a dead tree in the park — just *there* — taken for granted.

I unzip my backpack and take out the envelope containing the eighty-nine pages of my unfinished novel, a two-page ending tacked on at the end, the only pages I've really ever liked. I sit the manuscript on the wooden bench.

Maybe someone who matters will read it. Maybe a famous editor will publish it. It might be popular. A crazy boy wrote it, they will say, and people will wonder what I was like and pass it to their friends, telling them the guy who wrote it disappeared.

I open the envelope and take out the last page — the

ending. I like endings because you can be overdramatic and huge, and you can cry as you're writing them.

* * *

Elliot was tired of running. He knew that the police and the few people he knew in this world were on to him. He knew that soon, the inevitable swing of the heavy pendulum would be back his way, that his luck had nearly run out, that a justice-obsessed ghost would be rattling chains in his brownstone's dusty attic. He imagined the newspaper articles, trumpeting his wealthy childhood on the Upper East Side, and his fall from grace, his conviction for murder. He would get no chance for redemption, he knew, with at least ten boys taken by his hand alone.

He was more tired than he ever imagined he could be because he hadn't accomplished any of his goals, goals that had been set out in elaborate journal entries from age fourteen onward. He hadn't written a novel and published it, he hadn't shown art in a gallery or museum, he hadn't gone to Russia or to Antarctica. He hadn't been able to find someone to love and live with, he hadn't learned to cook properly, he hadn't even been able to support his elderly mother.

All he had left was his love of the city that he had always called home. And he would ask the city to relieve him of life soon, too. He was set on ending his life here — amongst the buried cobbles and tracks of streetcars, of flaming ladies falling out of burning buildings — because he thought a death in New York was important. He could jump from ten different bridges or swan dive from a 100-story building. What made sense for him, though, was to die at the mercy of a subway train. He would not change his mind.

* * *

I hear a train coming in the distance — gently rumbling toward the station. I slip the ending back in the envelope and leave it on the bench, then I walk to the edge of the platform, past the yellow strip of textured plastic tiles that let people know to be careful not to fall onto the tracks. I think of Elliot. He never had the chance to know what it was like to be happy.

The train races into the far side of the station, so monstrous it makes the entire platform vibrate.

I close my eyes and lean forward. I can't get arrested. I can't go to jail. I'll never make it. I jump down onto the tracks and stand right between the rails facing the oncoming train. The headlights are blinding me as the train rushes closer, closer, no time to think.

"Kurt!" Someone calls my name. It's Billy.

He's been following me. I should have figured he didn't trust me. "*What* are you doing?"

Isn't it obvious?

The train just twenty-five feet away, I can see the conductor's face — total dread. Seeing his face fills me with regret so strong it feels like I've drunk a thousand cups of coffee. I don't want to die. It's too early. I'll salvage my life. I'll find my way out.

It's too late to climb back up to the platform. I'll get my legs chopped off. I drop down as fast as I possibly can and lie flat in the foot-deep trough between the rails.

"Kurt!" Billy screams. "Hurry!"

I cover my eyes and force my body down as hard as possible to the ground, my back soaked by filthy rat-shit-infested warm water that pools in the two-foot wide canal. Holy shit. The train is here! I clench my jaw and tighten every muscle in my body.

The train barrels over me. It's the loudest sound I've ever heard — the power of machinery and metal and weight. Toxic dust makes my nose and throat sting instantly and the brakes emit a deafeningly high-pitched squeal as the conductor tries to stop the giant train.

It finally grinds to a stop and the electric engines shut off. The station is totally silent.

I slowly open my eyes. I move my hand up to my face to make sure I'm not bleeding. I'm still alive. I can see up through the connection between the cars.

Billy squints his eyes, looking down on me, afraid of what he's going to see, I think. His face betrays a look of relief so profound that I know he'll always care about me.

I lift my head up slightly and wave, so he knows I'm okay.

"He's alive!" he screams and starts crying instantly.

I exhale, realizing that I've been holding my breath for a long, long time.

The conductor runs down the platform toward me. I can hear his footsteps. He spots me, a confused look on his face, and climbs down between the cars pointing a flashlight at me. "Are you alright?" he asks nervously.

"I think I'm going to be okay," I say.

And I really do.

ACKNOWLEDGEMENTS

Thank you Don Weise, Scott Coffey, Eric Myers, Paul Bravmann, and Kim Fay for your help and talent.

Thank you Spencer Krug and Sunset Rubdown, Adam Rapp for *Red Light Winter*, which was inspiration for the setting and some of the vibe of this novel, and all my friends in New York City. Thanks to the members of my writing workshop (John, Paul, Robert, Mike and Matt) for help in the early stages of writing this story.

Also, thanks to Jon Anderson and Greg Jones at Running Press.